The Glow of Christmas

A Tangle of Truths, Chaos, and Christmas Not So Long Ago

MAURICE BROSNAN

Disclaimer

All events, characters, and stories in this book are entirely fictional. Any resemblance to actual persons, living or deceased, or real events is purely coincidental. The characters, places, and incidents are the product of the author's imagination, and any similarity to real people, places, or events is unintended.

Copyright

The Glow of Christmas

The stories are drawn loosely from memory and imagination. The line between the two is not always clear, even to the author.

First Edition: 2025

Published by Clonmore Publishing

ISBN:978-1-0369-6849-6

Dedication

To the glow of old Christmases — to the laughter, the rows, the Forty-Five drives, the broken toys; to the turkeys, the prayers, the postmen, the hunt, and the poker — to those who came and those who went.

To my mother, the peacekeeper, with her Holy Water — "Jesus, Mary and St. Joseph" — and the faith she kept in us.

To my father, with his paper and his poker by the fire — his bark always worse than his bite.

To my family, uncles and aunts, whose stories and bits of stories I still hear: *"I remember forty years ago…"* — and then some truth or tale would follow. They might have thought we weren't listening, but we were.

To my wife, my children, and my grandchildren — may you all have as many happy Christmases as life will give you.

Some are gone now, but none forgotten.
To me, they are still part of every Christmas.

Preface

Christmas was never one thing. It could be comic or cruel, noisy or still, full of neighbours or full of ghosts — and sometimes all of that in the one day. In our house, laughter and voices ran high, and peace followed only when the noise ran out.

The Glow of Christmas, as I remember it, was not the shine of shop windows but the light that came from people — the faces around the range, the songs in the hall, the quiet hands that made do when money ran short. There was holiness in it too, though half of it went unsaid: a mother flicking Holy Water into corners, a father behind his Paper, certain of the price of cattle and the will of God in the same breath.

This book is not a history, nor a sermon, nor a confession. It's a tangle of truths — part memory, part imagination — drawn from the voices and faces that filled my young world. The times were hard, but people were harder still, and not always in a bad way. They laughed loud, forgave slowly, and bore more than they ever said out loud.

You'll find the whole parish here if you look close enough — the card players, the mischief-makers, the worriers, the wise women, and the eejits who thought themselves both. Some stories will give you a laugh, others a lump in the throat. That's as it should be. Christmas itself was never built from comfort alone.

What I've tried to catch is the flicker — that human light that glowed through the chaos of it all. The turkey plucking, the fox hunts, the prayers and pints, the small acts of mercy that held a community together when the world outside was changing faster than we could catch our breath.

The nights are long, but the stories are warm. Some will make you laugh, some might sting a little, but all of them, I hope, will remind you of something true — that in every dark winter, there's still a glow to be found.

Contents

The Púcá and the Poker

Before Christmas ever showed its face, there was Halloween — the true start of winter. That was when the dark began to whisper, and half the parish claimed to hear things best left unmentioned. Turnip lanterns flared in windows, shadows twisted on the walls, and every creak of the gate was blamed on the Púca. It was the season when stories grew legs, and faith had to share the night with fear

I remember one Halloween night as clear as yesterday. I was about eight, I'd say. The clocks had just gone back, and the darkness came in early, sulky and mean. My father followed the forecast as faithfully as he followed the Angelus, and not a syllable had been said about storms. But that evening, the sky took a turn; clouds, black as the ace of spades, smothered the last bit of light. Twas hard to put a finger on it, but there was something in it that didn't feel right; it wasn't just weather. It was something else—quiet, heavy, wrong in a way that made the dog creep under the table and stay there.

Our kitchen was "lit" by a single bulb hanging from the ceiling, though you'd be hard pressed to prove it. Lit was a generous word—any decent candle would have shown more backbone. Shadows clung to the walls like wallpaper peeling at the corners but refusing to come down altogether.

Halloween, All Saints, and All Souls — three days welded together, heavy as stones in a pocket. They carried a weight in our house, for it was said the dead were on the move then.

White candles flickered in the window — half comfort, half warning.

I didn't grasp the full meaning back then, but I knew enough to keep every toe tucked under the blanket at night — just in case some wandering soul came sniffing round for a nibble.

Mother moved around the kitchen with her bottle of Holy Water, flicking it into corners as if she were shaking crumbs off the tablecloth.

"Jesus, Mary, and Saint Joseph protect us from all harm," she said—firmly enough to frighten a banshee. Then, softer, almost like she was speaking over the garden wall to someone she knew well:

"The light of Heaven to their souls."

She gave a last shake toward the hearth and stood back with the air of a woman who had the whole world, seen and unseen, put in its place.

My father was planted by the fire in his súgán armchair — the one he'd cobbled together himself out of stray bits of ash and oak from the barn. A throne of sorts, though you wouldn't dare call it that.

He had the *Examiner* spread across his lap like a shield, half-listening to us, half to the wireless, and half to neither. Now and then, he'd drop one of his sayings, casual as you like, the way mash is flung to hens.

"Paper never refused ink," he'd mutter, without lifting his head. Or, with a frown, "Always read between the lines."

We never knew if he meant the headlines, the neighbours, or ourselves — but the message was plain enough: use your loaf, and don't swallow everything you hear.

And the wireless itself — Lord save us. Ours was a Pye, with a fine mahogany case and four knobs: on/off, volume, tuning, and another that was supposed to switch between long and medium wave, but mostly did neither. A temperamental yoke if ever there was one.

The aerial was nothing but a length of wire dragged out the back kitchen window and tied to a rusty rod stuck in the ground. And before you think we had a big house and two kitchens and bigger notions—don't. That so-called 'back kitchen' was really just a flat-roofed extension with a concrete ceiling that sweated water in fat drops. You could say we had a shower before we had a shower — only ours dripped straight from the ceiling.

The reception was cat melodeon at the best of times, and when it turned bad, they said it was "atmospherics" — pressure, isobars, cyclones, anticyclones. (And didn't we have an auntie Cyclone ourselves, twice as fierce as the weather.)

I remember once when the Taoiseach himself was on the wireless — something of great importance, you'd swear, by the serious heads on my parents — and the reception was gone to hell. Crackling, spitting, every word swallowed. The father lost patience and sent me out to hold the aerial rod like a fool.

So there I stood, half-frozen, staring into the dark, wire in my fist — and not a sinner to hear me complain. It reminds me of the verse from The Rime of the Ancient Mariner:

Alone, alone, all, all alone,
Alone on a wide, wide sea!
And never a saint took pity on
My soul in agony.

To this day, I don't know if it improved the signal one bit — or if the father just wanted peace inside.

But the real high pressure wasn't the atmospherics outside at all — it was inside the kitchen, with a bunch of

eejits tearing around like dogs chasing their tails. My mother was nearly demented, flinging Holy Water — Knock or Lourdes, she wasn't fussy — into every corner, wondering where it had all gone wrong.
God knows, she could've done with a gallon of the stuff, the crowd she was dealing with.

Through the crackle of the wireless came the ghost stories. Jack O'Lantern. The Fear Dearg. And the one that would keep a lad awake till morning — the Púcá. The voices rose and fell through the static, like warnings carried along the wires.

The Fear Dearg, so they told us, was the Red Man. But to my young head, he was no different to Foxy Donie after a week in Ballybunion. He went every summer for his dip, and he'd come back boiled alive, red as a rash, crankier than a sore bull.

Even the Mother of Sorrows — you know the type, the long face of misery—never happy unless she was predicting the worst — even she might have flinched at those stories—a woman who'd find doom in a rainbow. "When God closes one door, He shuts another," was her way of cheering you up.

But the Púcá — ah, he was the boyo that seeped under your skin. Sly, slithering, a shape-shifter with no loyalty to man or beast. He could turn goat or hare or black horse, depending on what divilment he was in the humour for. And if you were foolish enough to follow him — well, that was the end of you—not dead exactly,… just gone.

Gone where? Nobody knew. And no one dared ask.

Just then, in the middle of the Púca story on the wireless, Uncle Tom arrived in through the back door — and I don't mean anything supernatural by that, in case you're getting notions. I mean, he literally came in through the back, his trademark pipe puffing out smoke like fog off a turf bog.

Tom had his own unusual ways — by day he'd go places in the car, but at night he'd take the bicycle, pitch dark or not. "That's when the other world comes alive," he used to say. "Night owls perched in trees, bats flying loops overhead, foxes off to some henhouse, and rustling in the bushes — be jaysus, you wouldn't know what's in there, and you wouldn't want to either."

He abandoned his three-speed bike against the porch wall and came in muttering about the cold and the state of the roads. "Full of potholes, and the council blind to the lot of them. I might as well be cycling over ploughed fields.

His Morris Minor wasn't much better than the bike — a biscuit tin on wheels, a pure crock if ever I saw one. It was faded black with rusty front wings and bird poo all over it from being parked in the barn under the grain loft.

Over the last two years, he'd replaced three back springs, fitted new plugs and points, patched a hole in the exhaust, and wrestled with a dodgy choke that constantly flooded the engine. And still, the thing coughed like an old man with asthma.

Tom, though, was a grand, big, grávar sort of man — warm, witty, a grin that took its time coming, and eyes that'd peel the skin off you. He leaned his backside to the Stanley range, and for a second, I thought he'd fire one up the chimney.

"Better out than in," says he, as if the Lord himself had given permission.

Then, without so much as a pause, he launched into a rigmarole about the Púcá.

"The Púca doesn't bother with doors," he said, tapping his pipe against the grate, solemn as a bishop. "No, he'll come down the chimney in a smoky draught, or crawl out of the flour bin with a belly full. Then he'll slide into the ear of anyone daft enough to fall asleep without saying their prayers. And once he's in — well, God help you, that's all I'll say."

We were wide-eyed, hanging on his every word, when suddenly he paused and lowered his voice.

"Once he's in — and I mean the Púca now — he'll do worse than any earwig. He'll rattle around your head till you're fit for the asylum. The Red Brick House, as you and I know it."

We stared like eejits, trying to look cool—unfazed. But truth be told, I hated sitting near the window. The trees outside were twisting themselves into knots — and I wasn't sure it was just the wind. The branches moved like Neily Gorman's belly after a savage feed of porter and bacon. And the shadows? I'd swear they were hiding something. Something you wouldn't want to meet on a road at night.

"By the way," says he, "did ye ever wonder, when you're chewing your curny cake, if it's raisins you're biting into? Herself baked one last week and I scoffed it down like a gorsoon. Next morning, she opens the flour bin — and out marched a parade of dusty white cockroaches, bellies on them fit to burst. I swear to God above, I nearly got sick, but it was too late then. What's ate is ate, as they say."

He puffed away, satisfied, and scanned us with a glint in his eye.

"I thought it was the Púca that came out of the flour bin?" says I, trying to be smart.

Tom didn't flinch. He tapped his pipe and shot back, "Did you ever think, young fellow, it might've been a very big flour bin?"

And before we could so much as laugh, he was off again. He had one more yarn before taking his leave — about an old woman who opened a letter and dropped stone dead on the flag floor from the shock.

"Whatever was in it," he muttered, giving us each a hard look, "killed her clane there and then. Cold, flat, stiff as a board — not a twitch, not a whimper.

The very next day, her long-suffering husband went running for help, and didn't he fetch three high-up priests to exorcise the place? Three, no less — as if one collar wasn't strong enough to handle it. Whether they were genuine priests or dragged out of a haybarn, who can tell? There's always a rake of jiggery-pokery when there's money to be made out of fear.

And that, lads, was only the beginning.

Down they came — the three priests. At least, I *think* they were. Starched white collars like horse haymes around their necks, heads solemn as judges, eyes wide and wild.

They went at the house like they were drowning the Divil himself. Holy Water flying left, right, and centre — soaking wardrobes, cupboards, chimney flue, even the poor husband's long johns (and God knows *that* was no harm either).

Lord, the racket they made! Latin, voodoo, or some mad mix of both — no one could tell. But they kept at it for hours, roaring and flinging drops till the wallpaper nearly peeled off the wall.

Just past the third hour came a whoosh and a groan like an oak limb tearing in a storm. Did you ever hear that sound? It'd freeze the blood in your veins. Anyway, the three of them swore blind they'd driven the thing out, sent it back to wherever it came from. And didn't the neighbours for miles hear the screeching and howling — slicing through the thatch roofs and stone walls alike?

The dogs tore off, tails between their legs, and Missus Lehane swore till her dying day her black cat turned pale and vanished. I never heard the bate of it before or since.

As for the husband — that poor useless luderamáwn — he never slept a wink for three months after. Lay there stiff as a corpse, two candles blazing on the mantel, one eye open, waiting for the curly finger of the lad with the hood and scythe to beckon him away."

With that, Tom folded his coat around him like a cloak, ready to go, and gave us his final warning.

"Mind yourselves tonight, lads. There's things out there that wouldn't think twice about calling in — and God help you if they do."

Tom paused at the door, dipped his fingers in the Holy Water font, and blessed himself — slow and deliberate — forehead, chest, shoulders. The way a man does when he's not taking chances.

Without turning, he muttered, low and spooky:

"And may they pass by your house without knocking."

Then he half-turned, voice sharper now, darker:

"And if you hear knocking… don't answer. Not till morning."

We sat there gawping at each other, dumb as donkeys, staring out across the whitewashed wall. The way he told it, you'd swear every word was Gospel.

And then he vanished into the night — or so we thought.

The light bulb, weak and all as it was, flickered once. The silence thickened. You could nearly chew it.

Then we heard him outside — giving out like blue blazes. Not to us. Not to the neighbours. But to himself.

Which was worse?

You should have heard him — muttering one minute, whistling the next, banging into something and scolding the sheepdog, then cursing the moon or maybe the wind. One minute like a monk saying his prayers, the next like a murder of crows in spring.

Had something gotten into him?

Well… remember what he said himself.

The father, my mother — we all heard him. We peeped out the window to see what had him gone so berserk, so out of character.

Half-wary, the night being in it, I ran from one window to the next, following the racket.

There he was.
Lord save us, the man was possessed.

And why? Because the minute he'd stepped out the back-kitchen door, it was gone — his bicycle. Vanished. Not a spoke, saddle, or squeak left behind.

I could see his shadow through the window, foostering around the yard like a man deranged — rooting behind mother's garden wall, poking round the cow stall, tearing past the piggery, even nosing into the turf shed.
And who in God's name would hide a rotten old bike in there, with rats and mice crawling like the F.C.A marching in Collins' Barracks?

The last time I'd seen anything like it was when our dog went mad with distemper — circling the yard, teeth bared, ready to sink them into whatever poor soul came near.

Then, out came Tom's flashlamp then — the old one with batteries deader than last week's fish from Fogart's travelling van. The beam barely stretched past the tip of his nose, yet there he was, swinging it about like a Garda on the beat.
And I'll tell you this much: if he'd spotted the mark of a single footprint, we'd have all been hauled in for questioning. Not by Tom, but by my father — who was forever warning my brother Jackie he would "find his level."
Not a carpenter's one, mind you — more like the gallows. An exaggeration, of course. Jackie was only ever out for a bit of devilment. But you couldn't tell that to the father or to Tom. Too ancient, the pair of them, to see the craic in it.

The truth was, none of us had stirred from the kitchen that night — not even to inspect the pigs, if you know what I mean. So no one could be blamed. And anyway, who in their right mind would steal his stupid bicycle?

Not after the day Tom came freewheeling down Pluckane Hill. The chain hopped off, the brakes gave up, and down he went like a man late for his own funeral — straight through a gap in the ditch and headfirst into a blackthorn hedge that hadn't been cut since the Rising. They found him hours later, thorns sticking out of him like a porcupine, roaring for holy water and iodine. My father swore Tom's wife was picking spikes out of his hide for a week after, and from places no doctor or undertaker should ever have to see.

Since then, the frame was bent sideways, the saddle wouldn't sit straight, and the bell only rang if you belted the handlebars with your fist. Who in God's name would steal a yoke like that?

Could only be… or could it? Perish the thought.

So off Tom went on Shanks' mare, muttering curses under his breath, the flashlamp bobbing with every step — the beam jerking like the bloody Púca himself was dogging his heels.

Where was I?

Oh yes—

Young minds, God help us, are more like goldfish than elephants. Whatever fear the Púca stirred up didn't last long in a kitchen full of tearaways with mischief in their nostrils.

The echo of Tom's curses hadn't cleared the front gate when mother's gaze found the fresh spit sizzling on her range.

Tom and that blasted pipe of his. Every so often, he'd let fly a gob just to hear it fizzle — same sound as Father Blake's lisp sliding through his false teeth at Mass. We nearly choked holding back the laughter, watching the poor man's dentures rattle while the whistle escaped, sharp as a kettle gone to the boil. Mother beside me, squeezing my hand till the blood stopped running, warning me with her grip to keep my trap shut.

"Filthy, ignorant behaviour," she called it. And she was right. Jaysus, what kind of an amádan spits on a range? She'd told him often enough, but it made no odds. He was too old a dog to learn manners. So she swallowed her fury — too much of a lady to waste breath on him — and turned her sights back on us instead.

And didn't the room fall quiet—a pause, like the stillness before a storm.

Then, just as quick, the mood flicked. Laughter rose again, for mother had hauled in the galvanised bath and perched it on a chair. Brimful of icy water it was, six apples bobbing like fat trout, some with coins wedged in their bellies — a hidden sixpence or a brass threepenny bit if luck was with you.

We lined up like lunatics, hands behind our backs, mouths as wide as Ballyheen piers, ready to dunk for treasure. Rules were simple: heads down, no hands, grab what you could with your teeth.

The place erupted. One by one, we plunged, came up dripping and spluttering like landed fish. The floor turned to a puddle, and the walls echoed with laughter. Mother — usually caught in the cycle of stitching, sweeping, scolding — stood back and smiled—a soft, rare smile, lighting her whole face.

Joe was first to nab the prize. Up he sprang, apple clenched in his gob, coins spilling on the boards like he'd struck oil.

"Big mouth," muttered Jackie, sour with envy. We knew well what he wanted the sixpence for: a sixth-class boy had promised him a stack of *Beanos* and *Dandys* for exactly that price.

"Go easy now, Jackie," mother warned, still gentle. "You'll have your turn. Wouldn't it be a pity to spoil the fun with bickering?"

But Jackie had the patience of a Jack Russell waiting on his dinner — and the temper too. He scowled: "Fool! I hope it chokes you!"

That was it — the last straw. Mother's voice hardened. "That word again! It's a mortal sin to call your brother a fool. You can tell that to the priest next Saturday at confession.

The air froze. We held our breath. Like statues, everyone. The same as Neily O'Leary freezes at the sight of work.

And then, as if summoned by God Himself, down went my father's newspaper. Slowly, deliberate as a hangman, he reached into the grate and drew out the red-hot poker. The tip glowed, smoke curling lazily into the air.

He didn't wave it. He didn't need to. The sight alone was warning enough.

We knew the rhythm by heart: my father, the enforcer, his authority as unbending as the iron in his hand. When he pulled that poker from the fire, we half-expected to be branded like cattle in the cowboy films. The scowl on his face, the slow lift from the grate — he might as well have been a sheriff laying down the law.

Order was restored for now. The poker pushed back into the grate; the hush held. Then mother drew the breath that could reset a room.

But beneath the noise and nerves, it was mother who held the real line. Thirty-six years she'd waited for her firstborn. Six years later, she had six tearaway sons. And here we were now — wild, loud, a house fit to drive Father Mathew himself to drink.

Still, mother wasn't one to throw the towel in easy. She let out a sigh — not just any sigh, but the one that froze us to the marrow. Shoulders dropped, eyes darted. We knew that sigh. It meant the game was up.

"Right," says she, voice low but steady. "That's it. Either ye straighten up and act like Christians, or the fun is finished. And don't come to me whining at Christmas.

Ye'll get nothing. Do I make myself clear? Nothing. 'Tis up to ye now, ye ungrateful pack of..." She stopped herself there for fear she might say something out of character. But she did make herself clear—message understood.

That quieted us. We chose survival.

So we tried to act respectable — like the Holy Marys up the road, butter-wouldn't-melt faces, born clutching rosary beads and half-ordained for convents or collar studs. You never heard a peep out of them, only prayers. They'd bless themselves if a dog sneezed. We mimicked them now, heads bowed, hands folded, eyes darting sideways to see who'd crack first.

The backkitchen door creaked. In walked Uncle Tom, covered in a cloud of smoke. I'd swear he never left that damn thing out of his mouth. Burned the eyes out of everyone. His own watery eyes swept the room: Joe's bloody mouth, the wet floor, Jackie crouched by the fire.

"What's going on here, gorsoon?" he asked Joe, sharp but not unkind.

Joe opened his mouth to curse, but thought better of it. Tom was holyish and wouldn't stomach foul language. "Bad language is the sign of a badly reared pup," he always said. And considering the half-crowns Tom had slipped him down the years, Joe swallowed hard.

"That fecker Jackie— the miserable so and so— swung the apple at me and cracked my tooth in two. Now my gob feels like a mouthful of thorny wire. He'll pay for it yet."

Tom didn't so much as blink. He drew on his pipe and said, calm as you like:
"Your father can file it down with sandpaper. Sure, it'll be grand before you're married."

Joe grumbled and slunk off to the back kitchen to wash his mouth.

My father stayed by the fire. His jaw was tight. He glanced at Tom.
"You and Esther don't know how lucky you are, not having a houseful of ruffians under your feet."

The words cut deeper than he knew. Tom's eyes softened, but he said nothing. He didn't have to. The truth was, he and Esther would have given their right arms for the chaos in that kitchen: even the bickering and the blood.

The silence thickened. Tom tapped his pipe against the range. To him, our racket, our fights, even our bruises must have sounded like music.

He stayed on a while, steadying the air. The fire cracked as a sudden draught shot up the chimney. Then the turnip lantern flickered, shadows jittering across the walls.

And without warning, a pale face pressed to the window. The glass rattled. A high-pitched growl rose outside, thin and inhuman.

"The Púca!" Joe screamed, clutching his bandaged gob.

Mother jumped, beads in hand, prayers spilling as fast as hailstones.

"Jesus, Mary and Joseph defend us from harm!" she muttered.

The father was on his feet, poker blazing in hand, ready to take on the Devil himself. He marched to the door, shoulders set. The face vanished. The growl died.

The door swung open. In strolled Jackie, the picture of innocence. In the commotion, nobody had even noticed he had left the kitchen in the first place.

"What's the panic?" says he, flashing a white cardboard mask from inside his jumper — his face twisted into a grin.

Mother half laughed, half groaned.

"So that's what you were at? You gave me the fright of my life, you pup."

Joe was fit to burst.

"You sneaky little fecker. Now I know it was you who gartered the cardboard box that mother blamed me for. You louser."

Jackie smirked, drinking in the uproar.

Mother shook her head, smiling despite herself.

"Ah, Joe, it wouldn't be Halloween without a good scare, now would it?"

Tom leaned on the doorframe and gave Jackie a wink.

"And it wouldn't be Halloween," says he, "without the Púca dropping by."

Laughter broke then — soft and shaky. Even the father, poker still in hand, let the corner of his mouth twitch. But the tension still hummed in the air.

When it ebbed, mother brought out the barmbrack. Treasures hid in its belly — ring, coin, rag, stick — prophecies in crumbs. She sliced it neatly, the knife scraping crums off the crust.

Joe found the coin and grinned through his bloodied mouth. Jackie pulled the rag in a subdued temper.

"Sure, 'tis only a bit of fun," mother said gently. "Be thankful for what you have."

Tom checked the clock and buttoned his coat.

"I'd best be off. Herself will have the lamps lit in the yard if I'm not back soon."

The father nodded. "Goodnight, Tom. See you the day after tomorrow for the graves."

Tom gave us a last look, soft and knowing, then stepped into the night. The door closed.

The father let out a long sigh through his nose. "Right," says he. "Get your rosaries. And not another word out of any of ye. I mean it now — no more tomfoolery."

Down we went — knees on the cold flags, elbows on chair seats, the rosary beads clacking away like hailstones on a half-door.

The father's voice was granite — hard, steady, unrelenting. The mother's was a softer thing altogether —

like butter left out by the range — slipping in under his, lifting the whole thing along like a tide.

By the second decade, the sting had gone out of us.
By the third, we were half-thinking of sweets and comic books.
By the fourth, only the mother's gentle lilt kept us from keeling over entirely.

Then came the Hail, Holy Queen — and you'd think we were done.
But no.
The father went off on one of his long, mournful litanies — the names of saints tumbling out like cattle down a boreen.

"Saint Joseph, pray for us. Saint John the Baptist, pray for us. Saint Aloysius, Saint Anthony, Saint Jude the hopeless case..."

And then he veered into the dearly departed — the whole parish, dead and living: parents, brothers, sisters, uncles, aunts, neighbours, and their neighbours' neighbours, and fellas we never even met.

He prayed for them all.
I thought he'd never stop.
I was nearly ready to ask Saint Christopher to pray for me — that I might survive it.

Then the last "Amen" dropped like a stone, and the father, without ceremony, said, "Off with ye."
We scattered like hens in the haggard, the floorboards groaning underfoot.

I lay in bed, eyes fixed on the ceiling, the night playing back in my head — the laughter, the rows, the face at the window, the chipped tooth, the blazing poker, the beads clicking through our fingers.

Downstairs, I could hear my mother's voice, low and musical, weaving through the father's deeper rumble. That was their way — calm after the storm.

By morning, the turnip lantern would be tossed to the dung heap. Joe's tooth would become a yarn, and Jackie's prank would grow legs like a good story should.

And I thought of the apple — how one poor apple had caused such ructions. Sure, hadn't apples been the start of trouble since Adam bit into the wrong one?

But lying there in the half-dark, the house finally settling around me, I realised something.

The madness, the fights, the scares — they weren't just mayhem.

They were proof of something solid.

We were alive.

We were a family.

And we weren't half bad.

Not bad at all.

Once the masks were packed away and the lanterns thrown on the dung heap, November took hold. The nights grew long, and the people went low in themselves. That's when the Forty-Five drives began — the first flicker of life after the darkness, where rows, laughter, and rivalry filled the gap between harvest and Christmas. If you wanted proof the parish was still breathing, you'd find it in the card hall.

The Hawk is a Quare Bird

Between Halloween and the big shopping day — the eighth of December, God bless the Immaculate Conception — the mood always sagged into a lull. The turnip lanterns were flung on the dung heap, the fires banked high, and you'd even swear the dogs were fed up with themselves — thrown down like false teeth in a glass by the bed. Some went low in themselves, others turned sour with the world. "Shake yourself up and cop on," they'd be told (as if that ever cured a soul). And that's when the Forty-Five drives earned their keep — a lifeline out of November's gloom, the first stirrings of life when the parish remembered itself again.

The hall was no palace (nor ever pretended to be for that matter). Corrugated iron outside, matchboard inside, and two paraffin heaters puffing out more fumes than heat — a death trap by today's standards, though nobody died of it that we know of, at least.

And if the fumes weren't enough to kill you, a blue fog of Woodbine, Sweet Afton, John Player, and Mick McQuaid clung to the rafters like a roof of its own.

Steam rose off the coats of men who had cycled miles in the rain, drenched till you could near wring them out and peg them on the line. 'Tis small wonder the coughs in the place were worse than a calf with the hoose.

On a trestle table at the top of the hall sat the prizes: a turkey — sometimes a goose if Mrs O'Connor on the committee had her way, for she reared more birds than she could ever get rid of — a ham, and a bottle of Powers or Paddy. I'd like to say they gleamed, but under the weak hall bulbs that'd be a lie. The prizes just squatted there, waiting to be carried off at the night's end.

We weighed those prizes in our minds the way other places weigh cups: Liam MacCarthy and Sam Maguire had nothing on a decent ham in December. And before any bird was strapped to a carrier and pedalled off under the moon like it had business elsewhere, there'd be rows enough to stock a courthouse.

Cards slapped; tables rattled. And if some wily old codger held back a trump, he'd let it down with a wallop that'd wake the dead. The greenhorns nearly died — 'twas like a baptism of fire — but for the rest of us it was the best craic of all. And if you got your chance, you'd love nothing better than to soften their cough a little.

Then came the real craic. Just when some poor divil thought he had the game in the bag, down would come the knuckles — thundering off the table, near frightening the life out of any innocent not reared for that kind of

carry-on — while a voice would crow:
"That'll put a halt to your gallop!"

A row could flare at any moment — and often did. Half the hall came for that alone. Accusations flew like sods over a ditch: "Bulking the cards!" (and devil a man there could define bulking if you put a gun to him).

Among the regulars was Séamus. By day, he cut timber; by night, he cut his teeth on the cards. He was well past forty and on the road to bachelorhood when a game of 45 turned his luck. One night's play landed him a job, and the job brought him to Cáit — a fresh-faced woman of fifty with apple cheeks and rhubarb tarts that could soften stone. They married quickly, for they had waited long enough, and neither had years to waste. From that day on, Séamus believed in Lady Luck as firmly as he did in the Catholic Church, considering it the one true faith.

Seamus' partner that night was Alice. Truth be told, she was never mad for the cards. What drew her out was the company, the hum of voices, the gossip spilling easily as porter, and the small comfort of knowing you were still alive in the world. You'd gather more in a single hand of Forty-Fives than in a whole week staring into a dead grate. Stay at home and you'd rot. Step out, and at the very least, you'd see some poor divil worse off in body or in spirit than yourself.

But Lord help her when she was paired with Mick the Hawk. His sheer bulk alone would frighten a horse, and the way he twisted and thundered was like something dragged out of the Stone Age. Near eighty, seventeen stone if he was an ounce, with a hide like old leather and tufts of hair sprouting from nose and ears, he was a quare bird entirely. He filled a bench meant for two, hammering his knuckles on the table till the timber rattled. His manners were no better than a bullock's; he'd sprawl across the table and belch out rules like a jennet squabbling with a stubborn donkey.

"God save poor Alice," the neighbours would mutter, "sure the Hawk would frighten thunder itself if it crossed him."

And there beside him sat Alice — a small, dunchie creature with her shawl pulled tight — shrinking further with every roar. No bigger than a dreoilín, a wren to you or me, and as quiet as the church mouse she was always called. She hated the very sight of a deck when the Hawk was near, for the man could turn a game of cards into a sermon — and a crooked sermon at that.

"Hold your horses there, young man," the Hawk thundered (and every horse in the hall obeyed). You followed with a heart when you should have played a spade, and spades were led, which were trumps. Now, if you had played the spade when you should have, you would not have it in your hand to take that last trick. So your hand should be decked and the game ours. That's cheating where I come from."

By the end of it, no one knew who had played what, only that the Hawk had claimed the trick and the game.

He could confuse a nation. Referees were slow to get involved, for there were so many sides to his arguments you'd want to be God himself to untangle them — and even He would be tugging at the collar. *"I've been playing this game since you were in short pants,"* the Hawk would bark at referee and opposition alike, and they'd retreat. Alice swore she'd faint dead away if ever she landed opposite him.

That night, she prayed she wouldn't.

Just when Alice thought she'd been spared the Hawk, in slid worse — Greasy Johnny with his shadow, Littlelump. He was so called because he was a tall, useless hoor of a man with a belly like a balloon from ating rashers of fat bacon and washing them down with porter. His middle, if you can picture it, was like a giant dough ball, only with ears and a mouth tacked on for the laugh.

The crowd shifted. Johnny was a tangler who lived out of a Bedford van, gone for days and back with a load of chainsaws, clocks, radios, old gramophone records only fit for the dump, and any other bit of junk he could lift. Off the back of one lorry and on to another, if you like — his own version of a supply chain, he had curly hair that bobbed when he talked, a beard salted with pipe ash and Guinness froth, a wad of notes bound with an elastic band, and a snaky grin of yellow teeth that'd make a pig ashamed of its father.

Séamus had no love for him. Years earlier, Johnny sold him a chainsaw that rattled itself to bits inside three days.

When Séamus went back looking for sense, Johnny only laughed. *"Buyer beware, Séamus boy. If old cows milked like young, there'd be no call for the bull."*

"If you sold me a shovel," Séamus shot back, *"it'd bend stirring stirabout."*

Littlelump said nothing, as was his way. He sat there, sallow as candlewax under an oversized cap, more cartoon than man. Some people said, more than one or two, he was the kind of snake who would sell his own mother if you wrapped her in brown paper. He smirked now from behind Johnny's shoulder, and the very sight of him was enough to sour the stomach.

Johnny grinned wider, sensing blood. "Tell you what," says he, loud for all to hear, "why don't we make it interesting? A tenner says me and the lad here skin the two of ye alive."

A gasp went up from a nearby table. A tenner was near a week's wages — and not every week at that. Alice's hands shook.

Séamus squared himself. *"Show me the colour of your money."*

Johnny peeled a filthy blue ten-pound note from his wad and slapped it on the boards. Séamus matched him without a blink.

"Come over here, lads," a voice called from another table. *"There'll be skin and hair flying — if I know anything about the history of these two."*

A whole table stalled their own game and pressed in close. The stage was set. An old bile was about to be lanced.

"Cut for deal and give over your blather," Séamus said.

Littlelump's fat fingers fumbled the pack, the cards bent and greasy from years of grubby paws. He dealt them out with all the grace of a man flinging turnips to pigs.

Johnny leaned back, grinning through his beard. *"No tokens now, Alice,"* he jeered, loud enough for the crowd to snigger.

Alice flushed scarlet, her hands shaking. "Séamus, I can't—"

"You can," he muttered, steady as stone. "Play your own game. Keep your cards close."

The first trick went to Johnny. He banged down a trump with a crack that shook the table. *"Your goose is cooked already, Séamus."*

A murmur rippled through the onlookers. Heads craned. Then, fumbling, Alice laid the Ace of Hearts.

The hall erupted — cheers, jeers, a bang of fists on timber.

Johnny's grin stiffened. The next tricks saw-sawed, one his, one theirs. The crowd pressed tighter, the air thick with sweat and tension.

From across the hall, the Hawk bellowed: *"Cold cards! Cold cards, I'd know it in my sleep!"*

Alice nearly dropped her hand, but Séamus steadied her with a look.

The game was now on a knife-edge, each card laid out like a blow in a prizefight. Silence fell — save for the slap of the cards and the wheeze of the heaters.

It came to the last hand.

Johnny leaned back, smug as a guinea hen up on a tree, yellow grin shining in the half-light. *"Well now, Séamus,"* says he, *"looks like Lady Luck's left you. Might as well hand me the turkey and your tenner."*

Alice's hand shook so fiercely that the cards near slid to the floor. The crowd held its breath. You could hear the wheeze of the heaters and the drip of rain on the corrugated roof. Even the Hawk had fallen silent, straining for the kill.

Johnny slapped down his card with a roar. Littlelump, puffed with himself, followed. All eyes swung to Alice.

Her lips moved in a whispered prayer, her eyes fixed on Heaven. Then, with a gulp, she slapped the Joker on the table.

The table rattled. For a second, there was dead silence. Then the onlookers erupted with cheers, whoops, and fists banging.

Johnny's grin froze, his face purple, ready for a stroke. Littlelump shrank into his belly, tugging his cap down over his eyes. Séamus nearly lifted Alice out of the chair with delight.

"Lady Luck," he bellowed above the din, "is a fine woman when she smiles!"

From the back came the Hawk's roar: *"Cold cards! Cold cards, the lot of ye!"*

"Go home and roast yourself, Hawk!" some old lady shouted back, and the place near shook with laughter.

Alice, fanning herself with her last card, gasped: *"I swear, Séamus, I'll never touch a card again — not till next week."*

Near midnight, the hall began to thin. Winners strutted out with turkeys and hams under their arms, losers gandered their way home muttering, but no man or woman regretted the night.

Johnny slouched at the side, his face twisted like he'd swallowed a bag of wasps, snaking away under his breath. Séamus wasn't the only one he'd caught in his time, but this night the crowd were glad to see him soured. Littlelump waddled after him, cap down, belly rolling like a pudding.

The Hawk, though, was still in full flight at his own table — loud as an empty drum. He couldn't care less what had happened across the room, only for his own hand, like a dog growling over his dinner. His knuckles thumped, his voice boomed, and the few left near him suffered his gospel.

"Cold cards! I'd smell them a mile off!" he'd roar like a mantra, and half the hall lost the run of themselves listening.

"Ah, clip your wings, Hawk, and give it a rest," a young lad shouted back. The hall burst into laughter, and the

Hawk snorted, scooped up his cards like crown jewels, and stamped out, the crowd hooting behind him.

Séamus gathered his winnings: a turkey and the filthy tenner. He walked home, happy and satisfied. Alice took her own road, her cheeks glowing from the night. Inside her porch, she dipped her fingers in the Holy Water font and thanked the Lord for giving her the steel to see it through — and, though the Lord himself mightn't approve, for granting her a small biteen of revenge.

At home, the fire was banked high, and a rhubarb tart warmed on the hearthstone.

"Well?" Cáit asked, eyes twinkling.

"Lucky," said Séamus, dropping the bird on the table and the note beside it, "lucky as a man could be."

He settled by the fire like a king, the smell of tart and turf thick in the kitchen.

So it went with us: once the turnip lanterns hit the dungheap, out came the cards — rows, roaring laughter, Johnny soured, the Hawk still acting the ghoul, a bottle under some lucky arm and a turkey or goose getting a midnight spin home on the bike carrier. Say what you like about Christmas—but make no mistake, 'twas the Forty-Five that set the foundations under it.

When the cards were packed away and the last prize turkey claimed, the air itself began to change. Even the frost had a sharper edge, carrying rumours of holly and tins of biscuits. November loosened its grip, and soon the talk turned to lists, letters, and the holy day that marked the real start of the season. Christmas was stirring, slow and steady, like a pot coming to the boil.

Christmas is Coming

Since the beginning, November has always been a month that tested every mortal soul. Grey, grim, and mean as a letter from the bank manager, it seeped into your bones and made a misery of the smallest job. The only purpose it seemed to have was to remind the body how short life really was — as if the man above, or the quare fella below, wanted us to remind us that we were never meant for this world.

The clocks were gone back, the evenings closed in tight, and summer had fled like a debtor dodging his dues. The trees stood naked under a cold sky, shivering in the wind. Smoke curled lazily from the chimney while down in the turf shed, the pile shrank like an old man's gums—each sod carted off by the cold that came at us from all angles.

Inside, the poor range crackled and spat, barely holding its own against the draughts that snaked in through the old sash windows. The window panes wept, their tears flowing down to form a pool on the windowsill. My mother hauled out every blanket and topcoat she could find to line the beds.

Come morning, the fire would lie cold and defeated in the grate, the chill clung to the sheets, and I could imagine my mother stirring us to see if our Souls hadn't taken a shortcut to Heaven during the night.

Mind you, this was in the days when electricity hadn't yet visited every house. And some houses — God bless us and save us — wanted nothing to do with it at all.

Molly Sheahan, from back the road, was one of those cursed with November. Starved of daylight, she'd fall into the crest of a slump the minute the clocks went back. Gone were the long bright evenings when she could ramble the roads without twisting your ankle in a pothole, and nose into every ditch and hedge and chew the fat with some neighbour until it twas time for bed.

"I hate November — sick to the teeth of it, I am," she'd moan, as if God Himself was to blame. "Nothing but misery and long nights in a dull kitchen, listening to my few old cows bellowing outside and rats — or mice, who can tell the difference — doing the Siege of Ennis in the rafters. There's only one cure: I'll go to my TD and demand the electric. And while I'm at it, I'll tell him to get the fecking holes sealed in the attic!"

Then she'd let out a sigh long enough to quench the old bit of fire that was left. "Sure, I'm the sorry woman now. I was afraid the electric would show up all the dust I never got round to claning. But blast the dust and the lot of it! By this time next year, I'll have light in the kitchen and brightness in my old head."

That was Molly all over: fierce in November, fierce with the talk. Come spring, she'd forget the rats, the ceiling, and the TD. She never did get the electric in, or the vermin out.

Truth be told, Molly wasn't the only one struggling with the change. Plenty of houses fought their own November battles.

And then December came, and with it a change. The gloom didn't vanish — not quite — but it softened, tilted toward hope. A flicker of expectation crept in unknownst. The old crowd said they could feel it in their bones.

That's when the old rhymes started up again, crackling from the radio, recited in the schoolyard, growing louder each day until the whole parish could nearly chant it in their sleep:

Christmas is coming, and the geese are getting fat,
Please put a penny in the old man's hat.
If you haven't got a penny, a ha'penny will do,
If you haven't got a ha'penny, then God bless you!

There was another verse too, for the sentimental sort, about bells and holly and giving more than you got — my mother down to the ground.

The papers were bursting with advertisements—turkeys, toys, tins of USA biscuits, chocolates, what to buy herself or himself for Christmas—Yes, indeed, Christmas was on its way, and there was no stopping it.

At home, on those long, dark nights, my father took up his throne in the súgán chair by the range, buried behind the *Cork Examiner* or the *Sunday Independent*—if there was still any print left in it after Jer's scissors had been at it—(I'll tell you later about that matter). The father would grunt now and then, just enough to prove he was still among the living.

The wireless played Bing Crosby's *White Christmas* like it was on a loop, and after the fifth or sixth go, my father had had enough.

"For the love of God," he roared, "turn off that fella and his infernal humming. We'll all be driven demented by Christmas Day!"

Mam didn't even flinch. She just adjusted the dial and muttered something about *manners and moods* being in short supply.

The rest of us battled at cards with my mother. And when the rows grew too loud — as they often did — she'd clap the deck shut and switch us to something less cut-throat: wrapping the presents.

She'd tie each parcel with a string and seal it with a blob of red wax. There wasn't much of value in ther presents, just handkerchiefs or socks or maybe a scarf—it didn't matter—Tis the thought that counts. Then, she'd stack them neatly in the corner and attack the mountain of Christmas cards. The glittery ones went to cheerful cousins and chatty neighbours. The Holy cards, stern and stiff, were for the pious souls already half gone to the next world.

By then, Joe's chipped tooth was barely noticeable, and the great Halloween row — over whether Jackie had walloped him with the apple or not — was history. In fact, the two of them had even formed a pact of sorts. They were like Santa Atheists, and their new craic was mocking the rest of us in our belief in the man in the red suit and his team of flying reindeer.

"Remember the lump of coal you got last year?" Joe grinned across the table.

"Yeah," Jackie muttered darkly. "Worst Christmas ever. That Santa — if he even exists — left me a lump of coal. Tight as a fish's arse — and that's watertight."

"You'll get a clip around the ear if your father hears you carrying on like that," my mother warned, her eyes still fixed on her cards. "And show some decency in front of your younger brothers. Don't be cruel."

But Jackie was never one to let a warning get in his way.

"Anyway," he went on, "Joe says there's no Santa. No Rudolf with the red nose. Brown nose, more like."

It was all codology to me—the nearest thing to a Pagan you ever heard. None of it shook my faith. Santa always came through. He always had.

And then, from across the room, came a roar.

"Who the hell is after mangling the bloody paper?"

We froze where we sat. The smirk vanished off the faces of the brave boyos. My father loomed over us, waving the tattered *Cork Examiner* like a judge holding up the Book of Evidence.

You have to understand—the Paper was sacred. He read it cover to cover: every last farming notice, every birth, death and marriage, cattle prices, horoscopes, letters to the editor, and even the cartoons—*The Lone Ranger and Tonto*, *The Better Half* by Bob Barnes, and anything else going.

But this day, the Paper had been butchered alive.

Billy, swept up in a tide of festive enthusiasm, had gone hell for leather with the kitchen scissors. Every advertisement with a Santa Claus had been hacked out and pasted into a copybook for his collection. There was glue on the table, scissors on the floor, and Santa's smiling face staring out from every page like a wanted man.

In his frenzy, Billy had sliced clean through the livestock prices, the letters to the editor, and even the blessed weather forecast.

My father's verdict was swift and final.

"If you so much as look sideways at my paper again," he thundered, "there'll be no Christmas in this house—and no

Santa *for you.* In my day, we had respect for our elders. You lot—ye're better fed than taught!"

And that was it. Billy's collection was finished. The rules were unspoken but carved in stone.

The *Cork Examiner* was the eleventh commandment: *Thou shalt not interfere with the paper.*

Like the Bible—only we didn't actually have a Bible in the house.

Still, the days ticked by, and soon the middle of December was upon us.

My father came in the back door, dragging a fir tree behind him. He set it into a bucket of sand beneath the Sacred Heart picture in the hall — one of the very trees he'd planted years before to shelter the house from the wind.

My eldest brother took charge of the decorations: fairy lights—the bane of our lives for the next few weeks. When one bulb blew, you had to test every single one, risking electrocution in the process, and of course the spares were always gone. Then came the paper ornaments, balloons, tinsel, and tufts of cotton wool to mimic snow. Streamers zigzagged across the ceiling, and sprigs of holly were jammed over the picture frames.

And when it was all done, my father—true to tradition—hoisted Billy, the youngest, up onto his shoulder to crown the tree with the fairy on top.

Jackie leaned back with his hands in his pockets and the smirk back on his face.

"She'll have a sore arse from sitting up there till after Christmas." he muttered.

He never saw it coming.

"And you'll have one now," growled my father, landing a clip across the back of his head.

"Ah, it was only a bit of fun," Jackie muttered, rubbing his scalp.

"If you don't watch your tongue," the father snapped, "you'll have no Christmas at all. Now, clear off the lot of ye, before I do something you might regret."

Jackie slouched off, mumbling curses, and when the air had settled, my mother stepped in, quiet as ever. She set the crib at the foot of the tree and gathered us round.

"One night before Christmas," she began, "a man was walking through a forest. He looked up and saw the stars shining through the branches, and it reminded him of Jesus, who left the stars of Heaven to come down to earth. So the man cut a tree and brought it into his home, as a reminder of that beauty."

Her eyes softened as she looked at each of us.

"Christmas isn't about what you get," she said. "It's about what you give and kindness and respect. If you live that way, people will respect you back. Jesus died for us.

Don't ever forget that. And like the man in the forest, always try to carry a little of that kindness into the world."

Then she blessed us with holy water, her voice low and gentle.

"May the Lord protect us from all harm," she said, making the sign of the cross, "and may the souls of the faithful departed, through the mercy of God, rest in peace."

By bedtime, the kitchen had changed. The range glowed, shadows danced across the walls, and the whole room felt like a haven in the dark. Christmas was coming. You could feel it in your bones.

The cards still lay on the table, scraps of wrapping paper smouldered in the range, and mother's words hung in the air like candle smoke, lingering, full of meaning.

But this was only the end of the beginning of the season.

Soon we'd be up before dawn, long pants and coats on and off to town for the Big Christmas Shopping Day. Not that we had much to spend — only what we had in our savings stamp book. But that was never the point.

The windows, the lights, the crowds, the wonder — it was all part of it.

And that little red bicycle in the shop window? The one I never dared to ask for? Well… deep down, I still hoped.

Once the talk of Christmas took hold, there was no stopping it. Lists were drawn up, pennies counted, and the great plans laid for the pilgrimage to town. It wasn't just about the buying — it was the seeing. The windows, the lights, the crowds, the chance to feel part of something grand. Even the poorest man stood a little taller on the eighth of December, with a few shillings in his pocket and hope lighting the way.

Christmas Shopping

Hope alone wouldn't get me the red bicycle, or much else either. My parents didn't have the money. All year I'd been saving what I could: a sixpence some weeks, a shilling if I was lucky, once or twice even a florin. I'd bring the coins to the post office and buy six penny savings stamps, watching the empty squares in my book slowly fill. By December, I'd filled one whole book and had the start of another, one pound, twelve shillings and sixpence in all. It seemed like a lot of money, but I'll bet it wouldn't even buy a mudguard for the red bike.

I knew I'd never have enough for a bicycle and would probably have to wait until I was shaving beside my father with his cutthroat razor. In my head, I could almost hear him saying:

"Wisha God helpmour little head, Gorsoon. A bike like that is only for the townies, not for our place."

And me replying:

"That's not foolish. Sure, hasn't Paddy Quane and Mick Mullaly a bike to go to and from work every day? And don't you have a bike in the barn? Sure, everybody has a bike."

And then him again, not very convincing either:

"Ye'd only end up fightin' over it, breakin' it, and patchin' punctures till kingdom come. By next Christmas ye'll be too big for the damn thing anyway—perched on it like a cat on a scissors—and it'll be flung in the corner with the rest of the notions. 'Tis neither the time nor the place for that carry-on where we live"

And then, as if to rub salt in the wound, or as daft Seanie once said, rub salt into the womb, he'd nail me with:

"And if you were seen cycling that bike down to the village, people would say you came down the river on a bike. They'd be thinking, isn't he the right gligeen of a young fella, not a scrap of sense, like a March hare."

Some of what he said made no sense to me. There wasn't even a river for miles around where we lived. And then I thought, *Give up. The townies, the lucky feckers, they get everything and give out that they have nothing.*

Anyway, the week before the big Christmas shopping day — the 8th December, the Feast of the Immaculate Conception, the shopkeepers' harvest, the day when the culchies invaded the towns and cities of Ireland — I took my savings book to the post office and cashed in over a pound. It felt grand, having it in my pocket, ready to spend on whatever I liked. It was my money, and nobody could tell me different. And sometimes if I got, a kind uncle or aunt, or a neighbour, might slip a few shillings into my hand and I'd say coyly, "No, no, thank you," but never too strongly in case they took me at my word.

It was only in late summer that year that my father bought his first tractor, a grey Ferguson 25. In came the tractor and out went his loyal working horse, sold off for the glue factory. Around the same time, Uncle Liam, a confirmed bachelor, treated himself to a new second-hand Hillman. It was a thing of beauty, with a red bench seat in front and a column gear change. He even bought two blankets to keep the front- and back-seat passengers warm and comfortable.

Whatever the car was like to drive in, it had to be better than the previous year, when I had to sit in short pants in the pony's trap, my nose streaming like a burst pipe and my legs turning such a shade of purple you'd swear I'd been steeped overnight in beetroot water. The blood wasn't just congealing, it was staging a mutiny, packing its bags and heading for the safety of my chest. Another mile and they'd have had to bury me along with the pony.

But that was only half the story. After what happened on our way home from town last year, my mother swore she would never again set foot in a trap drawn by a nervous, daft pony.

Wait till I tell you what happened!

You see, Pluckanes's steep hill was a treacherous spot for any pony and cart, whether it was loaded with churns for the Creamery or a trap full of passengers. A limestone quarry ran along one side of the freshly stone-chipped road, with a sheer drop just beyond the ditch. The ascent wasn't so bad. It was the downhill that spelled trouble, as the smooth stone chips left a pony's iron shoes sliding and scratching as if on black ice.

And then it happened: some rabbit or hare darted across our pony's path, as it was already struggling to stay on four legs. Well, you should have seen the pandemonium. The old pony bolted downhill in a terrible fright, though not as bad as the fright we all got inside the trap, it rocking and wobbling back and forth and sideways.

My poor mother was in a terrible state altogether. How she managed to get her rosary beads and Holy Water from her handbag, I'll never know. You know how it is with all the stuff they stuff into handbags, and all this while the pony was heading for the quarry and we to our certain deaths.

But then the Almighty intervened after my mother's quick intercession. Wasn't it the luck of God that Jack Dorney happened to be coming from the village in the opposite direction to us? I'll tell you this, people used to say that man was slow, but there was nothing slow about him that day. Seeing our runaway trap, didn't he pull his own horse and cart broadside across the road, risking his own life and limb, and force our pony into the ditch, sparing us from… well, I can barely think about it to tell you the truth.

The end of it all was that the poor old eejit of a pony ended up knotted in its own tackling, but we were alive. Barely!

And it nearly didn't end there either. Didn't the heavens open then, lashing down rain till it would drown a duck, and my father went home coughing and spluttering like a pair of bellows with a hole in them. Sure, by the following week, he was flat on his back with a bout of pneumonia. By all accounts, he was lucky to see out that Christmas. Lucky for him, and luckier for us — for if he'd gone, I can tell you, there'd have been no presents and no turkey, only cold cabbage and the neighbours shaking their heads at the wake.

But in the end, as they say, all's well that ends well — like the old woman scratching herself. Apart from the pony, there were no injuries, except to our pride, and sure that could do with being taken down a peg. The be-all and end-all of it was that my mother swore she'd never again set foot in that contraption, especially with a daft old pony between the shafts.

Come to think of it, isn't it peculiar all the same that a trap should be called a trap? And then there's a trap hiding inside the word *contraption* as well.

I'm straying too far from where I started.

At long last, the morning of the great Christmas shop arrived, and I was fair hopping with excitement, waiting for Uncle Liam to come rattling through the gate in his shiny new second-hand motor car. But sure, as the saying goes, there's many a slip between the cup and the lip.

By the time it wheezed up to our gate, the "new" had long since gone out of it. It was coughing and clattering like a blacksmith's forge, one headlight gone altogether, the other blinking like a candle in the wind, with a half pint of rainwater splashing inside for good measure.

When he finally drew the second-hand car to a halt, the shine was well gone. There he sat behind the wheel — a cranky old head under the Sunday hat, a crumpled suit that had seen one wake or wedding too many, and a Horrocks shirt with a Robin Starch collar sharp enough to cut your throat.

Didn't he then start hootin' the horn — one, two blasts, a pause, then one, two again — like a man drawing attention to his time keeping. It drove my mother demented. She'd been up since dawn and was in no humour for that fella tormenting us all before he'd even opened his mouth.

From the doorway behind me, she let out a long sigh — the kind that'd sour the morning's milk.
"That fella," she said, "has neither chick nor child to bother him. No cop-on whatsoever. Get into the car, boys, before he blows a fuse."

Out shot my brother Billy, nearly taking' the door off its hinges, and flung himself into the back seat. Lord God, you should've seen the look Uncle Liam gave him — I'd swear it upset his balance for the rest of the day. I followed more careful, easin' myself in beside Billy, tryin' not to rattle the man any further.

My mother came next — slower now — pausing at the door to sprinkle Holy Water on those she was leavin' behind, and on the lot of us already wedged inside. Then, after tendin' to a sick cow in the yard, my father appeared, wiped his hands on his coat, and slid into the seat beside Liam. The two of them no sooner settled than they were away, chewin' the cud over whatever was ailin' the world that week — as if the fate of nations rested between them.

Liam kept a small statue of St Christopher — the Patron Saint of Travellers — glued to the dashboard of his motor car. He was into his middle years now, cranky with it, and couldn't abide the faintest peep from the back seat. In his world, children were better seen than heard, and even that was pushin' it. Every few seconds the rear-view mirror sent back a glare fierce enough to light a fire with wet kindlin'.

The roads were quiet that morning. Bare trees opened the view clean across the fields. Near Jamesie's Bridge, I spotted a farmer bent under a great bundle of hay, a two-pronged pike stuck through it, his sheepdog trottin' close behind. The hungry cattle followed in single file until he found a dry patch and flung the hay wide on the ground.

Traffic was scarce — only the odd horse and trap (and I don't mean the horse was odd, you know yourself) — along with a few hardy lads pedallin' the same road. Just as well, too, considerin' Liam's habit of swingin' wide whenever he met man, woman, beast, or contraption.

At the junction for West End, I'd say his foot never even met the brake, for he drove straight into the path of an oncomin' van. My mother's hand shot out, grippin' the seat in front.

"Jesus, Mary and St Joseph," she gasped.

Liam muttered somethin' — and I could've sworn it was "Whee, you wretch!" — as if he still thought he was drivin' a horse and trap instead of a motor car. He wrenched the wheel at the last second. The van's horn blared, the driver's fist shot up, and his face went scarlet with rage. Billy and I turned our eyes to Heaven, but my heart was still hammerin' like a bodhrán. .

"If we see home alive this evenin'," my mother sighed, "it'll be only by the grace of God and St Christopher."

Even then I used to wonder: how in the name of God did St Christopher land the job of protectin' motorists, when there wasn't a motor car in the world when he was alive? He never drove one himself, but he must've seen some quare sights since he got the appointment.

Uncle Liam parked the car on Church Street — always facing for home. Said it made for an easier getaway, though God only knows what he thought he'd be escaping from — the shops, the crowd, or the price of things. More likely he was just a homing pigeon by nature.

Off he went then about his own business — free as a bird, and without so much as slipping a few shillings or a half-crown into my fist. No doubt he had "urgent matters" to attend to. Before long, he'd knock across a few like-minded cronies, each with a sop of hay from the summer meadow between their teeth, chewin' over whatever was troubling them that day.

I could nearly picture them crownáwning away about their aches and pains, the tablets they were on, and what ailment was next on the list. My cousin said once that Liam was on so many tablets himself — one for this, one for that — he could've opened his own chemist's shop. *Pharmacy*, they call it now, though it's the same dose by any other name.

Anyway, that was the last we saw of him till the journey home.

I tagged along with my father, while Billy clung to Mother's hand as they headed off for the shops. On the street, old friends who hadn't met in an age were shaking' hands and falling straight into the news of the day — the usual litany of health and weather, births and deaths, marriages and scandals, who was abroad, who was home again, and who they wished hadn't come home for the trouble they'd be causing and half a dozen twists in between.

Outside Leahy's Stores, two large women were talking over one another, each bursting to get her own bit said. They were wrapped in heavy gabardine coats — the height of fashion that year — and on their heads perched hats pinned down with hatpins long as six inch nails. One of them had an empty message bag hanging from her arm, while a wearisome child tugged at her coat-tail, desperate to draw her eye to a doll in the window.

"Come on, Mam, come on," the child whined, pulling without let-up.

"Will you hold your whist and be quiet?" the mother snapped.

"But you promised, Mam."

"The only thing I'll promise you, miss, is a good hiding. Be careful now — I'm warning you."

The other woman gave the child a look. "Is she your youngest?"

"She is, wouldn't you know it."

"And how many is that now?"

"I'm like an old hen — 'tis a full clutch I have. But I'll tell you this, and I told himself as well: there'll be no more clucking from me."

"Ah, you've been saying that every year," the friend laughed. "You never know."

"Go on out of that," said the first, "before this one drives the heart crossways in me. I told himself I'd meet him for lunch, so I'd better not be late — he suffers fierce with the old constipation this time of year. The divil can't pass a pub."

"God only knows where my own fella is," said the friend. "They're all the same once you loosen the reins."

All the while, the pouting child kept tugging until she nearly tore the sleeve off her mother's coat.

"Sure her father has her spoiled rotten," the mother said. "Daddy's girl, Daddy's pup, more like." She gave a shrug, as if that excused her altogether.

At last, worn down by the bawling and pulling, she gave in.

"Listen here," she said, "I'd better be off before this one drives the heart clane crossways in me. Have a good Christmas — and don't be adding to the clutch."

"Indeed, there's no fear of that," the other replied. "You know the saying: fool me once, shame on you; fool me twice, shame on me."

The two of them laughed and parted, the long-sufferin' woman dragging her screaming child behind her. The child's head screwed around for one last glimpse at the doll of broken promises.

My father had little taste for Christmas shopping. He had only a few items on his list: a bottle of linseed oil for the horse's tackle, a file and a rasp for his mending and fixing, and an all-important call to Mannion's for the final fitting of a new suit.

We stepped into Leahy's Stores — the big hardware shop in the heart of Church Street. As we pushed through the double doors, the bell gave a sharp clang that echoed through the place, announcing our arrival to the men in their brown coats. One of them — or maybe he was the boss — peered over his spectacles like a schoolmaster marking attendance. His pupils rolled skyward till only the whites were showing. He had the look of an undertaker about him, measuring every soul that came in the door for a wooden suit to lie six feet under — and he'd near have the tape drawn before you reached the counter.

A draught from the timber yard swept through the doorway, and the paraffin heaters puffed bravely against it, losing the battle by the minute.

The shop seemed enormous to me then. A shaft of dusty sunlight slanted through the fanlights above, as if the Lord Himself had peeled back the clouds to send down a blessing on the commerce below. Footsteps echoed across the wide boards as customers went about their business.

Immediately to the left of the door sat the little cash office — part confession box, part sentry hut — where not a coin or note escaped without inspection. Beyond it, the counter ran up one wall, across the back, and down the other, broken only by a small hinged flap for entry.

In the middle stood a fine display — cookers, oil heaters, and bits of furniture, all neatly arranged for admiration. Behind the counter, shelves and drawers climbed from floor to ceiling, three and four deep — a kind of hardware apothecary — each drawer crammed with nails, washers, nuts, screws, and bolts. Above them, more shelves groaned with the tools and treasures of the day: mowing-machine fingers, balls of binder twine, bottles of linseed and paraffin oil, puncture kits for bicycles, and a row of cast-iron Bastable pots and pans. Mirrors and pictures dangled from rails high up on the grey walls, catching the light when the door opened.

Every few minutes, a bell rang somewhere overhead. I was puzzled at first until the mystery revealed itself. The place was fitted with a Lamson Wire Cash Carrier — the height of modern ingenuity. A little carriage with a detachable cup ran on pulleys strung high across the shop, fired between the counters and the cash office by way of a spring-loaded catapult. Each ring of the bell meant the thing was on its way or just landed. I longed to be old enough to work there, if only for the joy of pulling that handle and sending it flying through the air.

It was the busiest day of the year. The assistants were bumping and jostling behind the counter, rushing to fetch whatever the customers shouted for. Drawers slammed, ladders scraped, and the smell of paraffin and brown paper hung in the air.

One of them I knew — a distant neighbour, sarcastically nicknamed Little John. He grunted and wheezed as the wooden stepladder creaked beneath him, reaching for the unreachable on the top shelf.

My father gave him a nod. "How's all the family, John?"

"The divil the fear of them," says he, leaning on the counter. "They're flying altogether — fit as fiddles."

"And yourself?" my father says, half-smiling. "You must be fairly fit too, with all your hurling."

"Fit, is it?" Little John straightened up, puffing out his chest. "I'll have you know I'm as fit as any man ever wore the Newcastle jersey. Check the *Kerryman* if you doubt me — my name's there most Sundays, putting balls in the back of the net against Castletown, Hazelwood, or Ballyglen. And come Sunday night you'll find me at Tim Twomey's dance hall, gliding across the floor smoother than a football on a Ballybunion wave. Light on my feet, so they tell me. Isn't that right, Mary?" he roared, loud enough for the cashier's office to hear him clear to Mallow.

Mary's face flushed as she bent over her ledger, pretending to write a receipt.

"I wouldn't know, John," she said, not looking up. "You're too busy blathering to let anyone else get a word in edgeways."

"Ah, come on now, Mary, don't be shy. If I took you for a spin around the dance floor, you wouldn't be complaining'."

"Maybe," says she, "if you learned to climb that ladder without all the huffing and puffing, I might consider it."

"Climbing that ladder keeps me fit!" says he. "And besides, you've a front-row seat here every day — you must enjoy the show."

Mary shot a look at my father. "That fella," she said, "would give a hare heartburn."

My father only smiled, leaning on the counter, and called out the few items he wanted to purchase.

Little John was in his element, sparking off the customers.

"I didn't think wild horses would drag you out on a day like this," he said, reaching into a drawer for a pound of four-inch flat nails. "All of them gaggling geese flapping about their Christmas shopping. I'll bet you the women only drag their husbands out to dip their little fingers in their wallets. Only for that, the men would be at home enjoying themselves. But I thought you were cuter than to be caught like that, so I did."

"I see you've your eye on the little cashier over there in the corner," my father said, half-joking.

Little John beckoned him closer with a looping finger and lowered his voice — or so he thought. In truth, he was half-shouting.

"I'll tell you this," he said. "On a day like today, you'd envy the lads in the Haggard Bar — no chick, no child, no claim on their few bob. And I intend to keep it that way for a while yet."

"John, my dear man," said my father, "I'll give you one bit of advice, and it's this: you're not exactly an oil painting. Don't keep that girl waiting, or she'll stray."

Mary, red in the face as any Christmas turkey, had, of course, heard every word. She threw a glare across the shop that would have stripped paint off a door. Little

John, realising too late, changed tack in a hurry.
"How's your brother up in Wicklow?" he asked quickly.

My father's brother, Paddy, had served his time in Leahy's years before and was now running his own hardware shop up there.

"He's doing very well," my father said. "Extended the shop earlier this year."

"Do you know something?" said Little John. "When I started here, I didn't know a bee from a bull's foot about hardware. Your Paddy taught me everything I know — right down to the spelling of every blessed item that comes in the front door or goes out the back. A man of great common sense, that fella. Do you know the first word he taught me to spell? Bastable! They were flying out the door like hotcakes. You'd be surprised how many people can't spell Bastable.

I'll never forget it."

He leaned over the counter and tapped a spot worn smooth by years of elbows.

"Look here," he said with a grin. "Your brother left his mark right there — his initials, plain as day — and even a rhyme to go with them."

Sure enough, scratched into the timber were the letters *P.B.* with the lines:

When I started, I couldn't spell.
By the time I finished, I did it well.

"Many's the customer leaned on that very spot," Little John chuckled, "never noticing what was under their nose.

Your Paddy always said that was his graduation certificate."

"Some people couldn't spell H on the side of a bag," my father said, leaving Little John scratching his head and staring at the carved rhyme as if it might explain itself.

Before the silence grew too long, the overhead carriage came whizzing along the wire, the bell giving its cheery ring to announce the arrival of my father's change and receipt.

Receipt in hand, we stepped back onto Church Street. The place was alive with shoppers — the hum of voices, the shuffle of boots, the clink of coins. At the butcher's, Christmas orders were being taken: a turkey for some, a bit of beef or a shoulder of boiling mutton for others — all carefully entered in the ledger behind the counter.

From O'Connell's came the smell of new bread; turf smoke curled from the little houses nearby, mingling with the glimmer of tinsel and the twinkle of a few Christmas trees in the shop windows. It was Christmas coming to life, right there on the street.

When we came out of Leahy's Stores, the father ran into an old friend, and that was the start of it. One word led to another, as it does, and before long the pair of them had found their second wind at the counter. You could hear the laughter spill out to the street — stories traded faster than pints, every one with a grain of truth and a gallon of exaggeration. It was the season for goodwill, after all — and for finding a reason to stay for "just the one."

Time For a Fast One

Leahy's Hardware had its own strange charm — the coming and going of customers, each with a bit of extra pep in their step; the faint smell of paraffin; the rows of shovels, pikes, oil lamps, and galvanised buckets; and the soft crackle of the wireless behind the counter. But the times were changing. There was even a display of record players in the window, with a small selection of records to choose from — no more of Granny's old gramophone. Only that summer, we'd smashed a load of her old records at home for want of something to do — the gramophone itself long gone by then. I suppose it was the work of an idle mind. Mother was right — an idle mind is the devil's workshop.

Still, I was glad to step back into the open air, where rows of wires straddled the street, hanging coloured bulbs above the shopfronts, their fairy lights blinking like stars. The street was busy, alive with a festive feel. Outside the Munster and Leinster Bank, the local school choir sang carols, their collection boxes jingling with the sound of pennies.

People stood around in little groups, chatting and laughing about something—or perhaps nothing at all. Yet not all could feel Christmas as others did; the bright faces and cheerful voices rang hollow to those burdened with sorrow, with empty pockets, or with the ache of loss.

A few children pressed their noses to Howard's Gift Shop window, staring at a little red bicycle displayed among the toys — the very one I had my eye on. I wondered if Santa might bring it to them, because he certainly wasn't bringing it to me. Our house always seemed to attract the mean Santa — the fellow who dealt in hand-me-downs. And hadn't I enough of that sort of thing, trying to squeeze into my brother's shoes, my toes already curling from the tight fit. The toys he left were pre-owned, pre-loved, and with very little love left in them, judging by their condition. It wasn't that our chimney was too small — far from it. On a clear night, you could look straight up through it and study the firmament in all its glory.

And then came the moment I knew my chances were banjaxed. A posh-looking woman — dressed like a mannequin that had fallen out of a shop window — swept up with her son to admire *my* bicycle. The boy was about my age, but you could tell he'd never seen a cowstall or a heap of dung in his life: fancy overcoat, velvet collar, mittens to keep his delicate fingers from the cold.

"Is that the one?" she asked.

"Yes, Mommy," he said, all clipped and proper, like he was ordering it from a fancy catalogue.

Right then, I knew I hadn't a hope. He was the sort who'd

be pedalling my grand red bike on Christmas morning — and have it tossed aside before the pudding was cold. I could see it all before me: the world neatly divided between the haves and the have-nots, and me firmly in the second camp.

Further down the street, my father ran into an old acquaintance, a man named Séan from Toureen. Séan suggested they go for a drink to catch up on old times.

If there was one thing I didn't want, it was to be stuck in some dingy old pub, listening to old men talk about old times. But then, had my opinion been asked for, it would have counted for nothing.

"Bring the gorsún there with you, Tim," Séan said.

Ah, wasn't it daysent of him all the same? As if I should be grateful, when I knew well I was nothing but an encumbrance — like a man trying to milk a cow on a three-legged stool with one leg missing. He'd have far better talk with my father without me hanging around like a bad rash anyway. And what else was I to do? Stand freezing in my short pants till I turned blue or wait like Finnegan's donkey outside the pub — patient, long-suffering, and ready to lug him home from the Creamery, his belly full of black porter and himself four sheets to the wind."

My father was never too fond of pubs. He didn't like "putting a slate on another man's roof," as he used to say. His sole indulgence was a drop of whiskey nightly before retiring to bed. "To keep the spirits up, you must put the spirits down," he'd joke.

He agreed to have the one drink with Séan, and that was all. The idea of lingering half the day in a pub didn't suit him; he always had his day planned. There was the important matter of visiting Mannion's Drapery, Outfitters and Haberdashery for the final fitting of a new suit, and it wouldn't do to have even a hint of drink on him when we got there.

My mother had said it was high time he discarded the old suit with the shine up the arse of the trousers. The fecking thing was fit for nothing except piking dung out of the cowstall. Besides, there was an upcoming wedding in the Midlands, and looking respectable was item number one on the agenda. One must show signs of prosperity, something to show for all one's slaving.

As I said before, the thought of going into a dingy pub and sipping lemonade held no appeal for me. But then Séan slipped me a sixpence and said,

"There, gorsún, get yourself a few gobstoppers. Your father and I will be in Eily's pub across the street when you get back."

I was easily bribed. I took the sixpence and headed for the sweet shop around the corner on Main Street.

What was it about those days when children walked around with their cheek muscles stretched to breaking point, trying to accommodate a gobstopper and flirting with lockjaw? Expressing yourself wasn't exactly encouraged back then. "Children should be seen and not heard," and "Know your place"—whatever that meant—were the mantras. Maybe that's why gobstoppers were invented in the first place. You know, I think I've solved it after all these years: a shut mouth catches no flies, or so they say.

But without expressing yourself, how would you ever know where that "place" was? Better out than in, as Tom proved the night he blew the fart up the chimney. And when, I often wondered, was the magic age when you were finally allowed to let out everything you'd been holding in?

With a gobstopper crammed in your mouth, there was nothing for it but to keep quiet and observe like a fly on the wall. Come to think of it, maybe that wasn't such a bad thing. There were lessons in restraint there: one has two ears and one mouth for a reason—look before you leap, and all that.

I had no sooner entered the sweet shop when a sour-faced, awkward-looking hulk of a man loomed up from behind the counter. He had woolly ginger hair and eyebrows as red as autumn leaves.

He was eating a thick slice of brown bread and jam, drips running down his fingers, which he licked off with his fat tongue. Eating while serving customers was not exactly suited to him.

"I'm in a hurry. What do you want?" he asked gruffly.

Indeed, I thought — though I kept it to myself. If he wanted my sixpence across the counter, he might have shown a bit more civility. So I asked for a red gobstopper from the jar on the top shelf — just to be awkward. There are ways of showing your annoyance without ever saying a word.

He placed his half-eaten slice — teeth marks imprinted on the crust — on the counter. Then, grunting and groaning, he reluctantly climbed the small stepladder to reach it. The steps creaked beneath his weight, and I half expected the ladder to buckle at any minute. Part of me even wished it did — the surly fecker.

Back on the floor, he unscrewed the cover, plunged his fat hand in, and nearly wedged it in the jar—a pity he didn't. I should've told him I'd changed my mind and asked for another colour, from the top shelf,—that'd have served him right.

Instead, once he retrieved it, he practically threw it onto the counter like you'd toss a bone to a dog.

"Is that all?" he asked as I studied the sour puss on him.

"'Tis," I answered, without saying thank you in return for his grumpy manner.

My mother had always taught me to say 'please' and 'thank you.' But there was a limit, for God's sake—and I had my own self-respect to think of.

If he'd worked on his customer relations a little better, he might have extracted a few bob more from me. As I said earlier, only the previous day I had cashed in my

Savings Stamp Book at the Post Office, and the coins were nearly burning a hole in my trouser pocket.

A whole pound was ready to purchase a cap gun—and a supply of caps, the very same one sitting on the middle shelf behind his counter. But with manners like his, he wouldn't see a penny of it. I'd take my custom elsewhere. More fool him.

As I was leaving the shop, I nearly collided with a woman coming in the door. She was dressed festively, with a sprig of red-berried holly on her coat lapel and matching bright red lipstick. In her gloved hand, she held a Consulate cigarette in a long holder — which, I imagine, she thought made her look sophisticated. Unfortunately, that air of sophistication vanished the moment she opened her gob and scowled at me.

"Watch where you're going, you little urchin," she snapped, nudging me out of her way.

I didn't know what an *urchin* was at the time, but I did know that an urchin I was not. Her voice was manly and hoarse, probably from the fags.

Then she crossed the threshold, and in the space of a few steps morphed into a different woman entirely — all smiles and sweetness.

"How are you today, Johnny, my dear?" she asked, loud and syrupy.

"My life is like an empty purse — no change," he replied, pleasant as you please, even finding a smile for her.

Well, what in the name of God was in the air all of a sudden? Your wan had gone through three personalities in half a minute, and your man — the big surly sourpuss — had turned into Mister Nice.

Curious, I paused just outside the door to listen. Well! I couldn't believe it. Words like honey dripped from his mouth, and the woman, whoever she was, lapped it up and returned the honey in spades.

To tell you the truth, it was pure sickening to hear after my experience with the pair of them. False as my Uncle Denny's teeth, they both were.

I could only conclude the woman—certainly, no oil painting herself—was getting along in years and wanted to drop anchor before the clock called time and her ship sailed.

As for your man, the big fecking galoot, he most likely wanted help in the kitchen, with the laundry, and whatever other benefits she might bestow. How else could you explain such false niceness?

I returned to the pub with a gobstopper threatening to burst through the side of my face. They weren't called gobstoppers for nothing. I often wonder how many sore jaws and crooked teeth were caused by those blasted things.

As I entered, the pub door screeched against the concrete floor and a dozen or more heads lifted in unison to see who was coming. I braved my way past the gawking faces to the far end of the bar, where my father and his friend Séan sat on high stools. I anchored myself on the stool closest to my father, hoping we would soon be on our way.

It was my first outing to a public house, and from my first impressions, I wouldn't be in a hurry to return. The place looked manky, with little evidence that the proprietor had entered into the Christmas spirit.

The last spring clean was probably done before De Valera and Michael Collins fell out over the Treaty.

Still, a faint effort had been made with the festive decorations. Tatty bunting sagged from the ceiling, interrupted here and there by a half-blown balloon inflated by someone's weak lung. A few sprigs of holly were thumbtacked to the shelves.

In the corner by the snug stood a half-bare Christmas tree, one side pared away completely and already shedding its needles. A few strings of tinsel clung to it as if thrown from across the street. The curtain facing the street was torn and reeking of smoke, and the window glass was smeared with cow shite from previous fair days.

The paint on the matchboard partitions was peeling, and the walls, once whitewashed, were yellowing, stained, and paw marked.

The ambience inside was bleak. The only touch of cheer came from a wood-and-turf fire, which threw out a little heat and half-heartedly smothered the smell of stale porter.

"Get that young man a glass of lemonade, Eily," I heard Séan call to the woman behind the bar.

Eily was a wiry-looking woman, past her prime and more suited to cutting turf in the bog than pulling pints. From what I could see, she held no charm for her customers, dressed as she was in a cross-over bib, her head crowned with a tuft of stiffly permed hair.

Her looks matched her personality. Without a word, she reached under the counter, poured a long glass of sparkling lemonade, and placed it on the bar in front of me. I removed the gobstopper from my mouth, wrapped it in sweet paper, and set it on the counter. It was still as big as ever—I might as well have been chewing a stone.
"That'll be eightpence halfpenny to you when you're ready," she said to Séan.

He fiddled in his waistcoat pocket and handed her a few coins. She grunted back something entirely incoherent. It was plain that being a publican was not the vocation she'd dreamed of as a child. Pulling pints, serving drinks, and listening to Paddy Whiskey wisdom in a dingy bar was more like falling into the trough of a nightmare than living the crest of a dream.

Séan and my father set about lighting their pipes, as if there wasn't enough pollution in the air already. I declare to God, you could hardly see beyond your nose for the smoke. Séan smoked ready-rubbed Mick McQuaid, whereas my father's way was more orthodox — almost ritual-like.

First, using the small blade of his penknife, he pared off fine slivers from a chunk of Clarke's Perfect Plug. It was the same penknife I'd seen him use to cut the roots of the young piglet's family tree, if you get my meaning — the squealing still rings in my ears.

He placed the slivers in the palm of his hand and rubbed them in a circular motion with the ball of his other fist until they were fine and flaky. Then he packed the tobacco into his pipe with his index finger.

Holding the pipe clenched in his teeth, he tried to ignite it — with varying success. Like a fireplace with a poor draught, it sometimes took several matches to catch. He would inhale and strike again, only to hear the pipe sputter and burn his finger with the curling match. "Bad cess to you," I'd hear him mutter.

When the pipe was properly lit — then, and only then — could a conversation begin. I've often thought pipe-smokers are more inclined to philosophy. The very process of inhalation gives them a split second to find the right word, punctuate their point, and synchronise the brain with the mouth.

The only thing that could disturb a proper parley was a watery-sounding pipe.

The pub's clientele was a mixture of townies and country people. The townies were mostly regulars, judging by their easy familiarity. The country folk were only passing trade, in town for the day, while their wives spent a few pounds in the shops for Christmas.

The place soon became overcrowded, and I dared not leave my stool for fear that someone would usurp it without a "please" or "thank you." I sat in a cauldron of smoke—Woodbines, Gold Flake, John Player, Mick McQuaid, Clarke's Perfect Plug, and turf from the open fire. My eyes watered, and oxygen was in short supply.

On either side of the fire sat two tall, lanky men, with their topcoats still on, imbibing hot whiskeys at a small round table. They were most probably twins, by the looks of them. They never exchanged a word and seemed entirely content simply to be in the company of others. Sometimes, I suppose, just being present, like a spectator at a good match, is as satisfying as taking part.

Then the back door from the yard opened. A boy about my age entered, bringing with him a swirling draught that killed the bit of heat from the fire.

"Blast it, will you shut that door, or were you born in a haybarn?" a man growled.

The boy's face reddened like the embers. He shut the door and hurried to a place near the two lanky men. Judging by his long-arched nose and lanky gait, the boy was clearly the offspring of one of the men standing by the fire. There was no storm the night when that apple fell from the tree.

The boy sat at a table, looking sideways around the bar, eyes up but head down. At one stage, he dragged his sleeve across his nose, leaving a snail-like trail to his elbow. Then, when he thought no one was watching, he pulled a cap gun from his jacket, pointed it at me, and pulled the trigger.

I smiled when his gun failed to shoot, probably because one of his watery snots had fallen onto it. I wondered if it was the same cap gun I had my eyes on in the sweet shop. Either way, I was not about to engage with the snotty little beggar, so I turned and looked in the opposite direction.

A pokey door beside the yard led into a snug, heated by a paraffin oil stove. The snug was mainly the preserve of women, who entered discreetly from a side alley. In those days, a woman in the main bar was frowned upon.

Still, some women rightly paid no heed to convention and took their enjoyment in the pub, albeit in the snug. On this day, though, it looked more like a meeting room or an office. Voices carried from inside, sometimes raised, sometimes sharp.

Once, the hatch opened and a hand emerged, circling in the air to signal another round. The hand alone told a story: smooth and soft, never hardened by a day's labour. It had never pulled a calf, spread dung, or piked hay. It was, without doubt, a pen-pusher's hand.

The bar counter ran close to the front door, where a rakish, scruffy-looking man sat cross-legged on a high stool. He was talking in an incessant monologue to a young fellow who nodded now and then, as if hanging on every word.

To my eyes, he was the sort who preferred talking about work to doing it—a man who knew very little about a lot, pontificating to others while too lazy to lift a hand himself; the kind that laughs at the next thing they are about to say even before they say it.

"Ahh, look who 'tis!" he said suddenly, referring to a big, heavy man, probably in the late twenties, entering through the creaking door.

"Sure, 'tis the Soprano himself."

The heavy man shouldered his way to the counter and called for a drink.

"Throw us out a pint and a whiskey there while I'm waiting, Eily."

His voice was high-pitched, oddly mismatched to his bulk. His trousers were filthy and tucked into his Wellingtons. His body coat, several sizes too small, was pulled together with binder twine. His hair was thick, woolly, and unkempt.

Eily looked him up and down.

"Every bloody time you come through that fecking door, Peter, whether 'tis hot or cold, you leave it wide open. You must have been born in a haybarn."

"You're not cold, surely, Eily. If you lived up the side of a mountain like me, you'd know what cold is. All ye townies are soft as butter."

Eily slid his whiskey and pint across the counter.

"Peter, 'tis no wonder herself upped sticks and left you.

Only a snipe could survive the cold and wet where you live."

"Ah, sure, Eily, I'm glad to see you're still your charming, tactful self and full of Christmas spirit. I bet you can't wait to rise out of bed every day."

They both sort of smiled guardedly at each other, and I took from the exchange that it was all a bit of fun. Nothing serious. Strange, the people you meet when you're out.

I kept my eyes on the snug. Now and again, Eily slid back the hatch, handing through a glass of sherry, a hot whiskey, or a pint of porter. The voices inside had softened; whatever row had started was now tempered by laughter and lubrication.

At first, it was fascinating to watch how well Eily managed the busy bar on her own. She seemed to know everyone's round, lining up porter and beer before the call even came. But as the crowd thickened, the strain began to show. Her face reddened, perspiration rolled down her brow, and her patience wore thin.

"Yara, hold your whist!" she snapped when a man tapped his glass on the counter for a refill.

The black stuff sputtered frothily from the tap, and tempers sputtered too. Customers complained about flat porter, or about ordering one thing and getting another. It was all too much for poor Eily.

She slapped a handful of coins into a customer's palm and turned to pull the next pint.

"You've short-changed me, Eily!" the man barked, puffing himself up.

Eily spun round, hands on her hips.

"Short-changed you? I'm no fool. I've been serving drink in this establishment since before you were in short pants, and never a complaint. I declare to God, if there's a man in Cork who would try it on for the price of a half-one, it's yourself."

A few customers looked around after Eily's outburst. By all accounts, she was not to be meddled with when she took the notion. A hush hung; you could hear Séan's pipe sputtering, loud as Uncle Denny's Morris Minor when he pulled the choke too far. Then, breaking the silence, a voice carried from further down the counter.

"Ah, will you listen to yourself, Jack. Don't always be as tight as a fish's arse. There's more to life than skinning fleas for their hides — God help you."

A muted snigger rippled around the bar — not the laughter of strangers at a jest, but the sly delight of neighbours watching old scores of some sort being settled.

Your man Jack — the one with the fish's arse — gave a crooked grin, pretending to take it all in good spirit, but everyone knew he'd try the same trick again in some other pub.

No sooner had that little misunderstanding been settled than fresh grumbles started up. The porter was flat, orders were mixed again, and the clamour grew louder.

Poor Eily was at her wits' end. Then, in the midst of her desperation, I saw her throw a withering glance and say something to a man seated at the counter inside the door.

He was working through the Cork Examiner crossword with a bit of help from his drinking companions. His hands, like the ones I'd seen in the snug, were also smooth and untroubled from physical exertion.

The man, it turned out, was Eily's husband. He bolted upright in response to whatever she hissed at him and shuffled outside to the backyard.

"Carry on there, lads," he told his friends. "See if ye can solve nineteen down and twenty-three across before I'm back."

When he returned, his arms were laden with turf and sticks for the fire. He collected glasses, swapped a few jokes, and stirred laughter. Then he took a quick spell behind the counter—boiling the kettle, washing glasses, stacking shelves. Finally, job done, he went straight back to his stool.

"The secret to a happy marriage, lads, is a fair division of labour," he declared to his friends.

You know how, at times when you think things can't get worse, they do. The pub door opened, and a small, weedy, runt of a fellow entered and sidled up to the bar counter. He had distinct, deep-set, evil-looking eyes and a wicked-looking head on him. A fresh wound on his cheek gave him a dangerous look. All taken together, this man spelt trouble.

"Don't make eye contact with that shagger," I overheard one man whisper. "He only came out of prison last week after serving a year. Broad daylight on Mallow Main Street, he put a man in the hospital—nearly killed him. That shagger won't be happy till he's back in jail. That's the type he is. His poor mother would have been better off if she'd squeezed her legs together the day he was born.

The weedy man slapped a pound on the counter.

"Give me a double Paddy there, Mam."

"I will not. You're rotten with the drink already. Clear off before I call the Guards," Eily snapped.

"I'm entitled to be served."

"Not in this house, you're not."

"I haven't had a drink all day. Go on, give me one for Christ's sake."

"Not while there's breath in my body. Now clear off."

"I know my rights."

"You lost all your rights the day you nearly killed that poor man in Mallow."

The pub fell silent. The customers either side edged away, leaving him alone in the glare of Eily's refusal.

"I'll sort this, Eily," her husband said.

He sat up from his stool, strode over, and without ceremony grabbed the man by the scruff of the neck with one hand and the hasp of his arse with the other. He frog-marched him through the door and flung him onto the footpath like a sack of spuds.

Eily's husband returned to his stool amid a round of applause. He did have his uses after all.

The snug door opened again, and I caught a glimpse inside. A troubled-looking woman sat with a glass of sherry before her. She wore a black coat and a hat held fast with a long pin. Her arms were folded tightly, her whole bearing defensive. From her demeanour, it was plain she was there on serious business.

Beside her sat a well-dressed man with soft, unworked hands, scribbling notes into a jotter—clearly a solicitor. Another man sat in silence, likely just a witness.

"The woman inside there, Tim," Séan said quietly, leaning towards my father and away from curious ears, "I know her. She's from back west, one of the Hennessys. My brother lives next to her. He told me the whole story."

My father nodded, drawing on his pipe. Séan shifted on his stool, elbows on the counter.

"They're a daycent old crowd, but don't take them for fools. Three sons she has—and a dead husband from TB. You wouldn't believe the trouble that followed her since the poor man passed away. Not an ounce of help did she get from his family, and she having three young sons to rear. In fact, it was the opposite."

He glanced at my father, his voice dropping lower.

"Didn't they try to claim some class of lien on the place, contesting the will? That crowd would do anything for money, greedy as hell. They should have remembered—there are no pockets in a habit."

My father exhaled slowly, smoke curling upwards. He listened but said nothing.

"The whole business turned bitter," Séan went on. "But she stuck to her guns. The case went all the way to the High Court, with that solicitor fellow in there representing her—and she won.

"The end of it was, her husband's people were saddled with all the bills, and it nearly claned them out—no better boys than the bigwig solicitors for separating a man from his money. One thing's for sure—that lot won't rush up them steps again. Serves them bloody right."

My father tapped his pipe against the counter. "Money is the root of all evil, isn't that what they say?"

Séan nodded grimly. "Three sons, and not a razor blade could slide between them. But when they grew up, more trouble came knocking.

"The eldest, Peter—a decent lad at heart, but a gligeen; he'd run with the hare and hunt with the hound. Talks a lot but says nothing; there's no substance there. He got married last year to a wan from across the county bounds, one of the Twohigs, the cattle dealer crowd. Good-looking women; they'd charm the birds off the trees—but behind it all, only gold diggers. They'd skin their mother for sixpence. 'Tis bred into them.

"Before young Peter knew it, he got her in the family way and was married post haste to avoid the shame in front of their uncle, the Bishop. The Twohig lassie made a pure fool out of poor old Peter. And once married, she turned him against his own."

My father drew on his pipe and released a ball of smoke.

"There's some people," he said, "who take everything, and never know when they've taken it all, or care even less."

"Well, last week it came to a head. Peter was helping his brother Richie clean out the well, and the whole thing flared up. Whatever bile was there, boiled over, Peter struck Richie with a shovel—near killed him."

Séan shook his head. "The young lad's in hospital now, stitches and a cracked pole. And the mother? She's in there with Clancy, the solicitor, changing her will. Writing Peter out of it. As far as she's concerned, he's made his bed, and he can lie in it."

A few minutes later, the snug door opened and the woman, the solicitor, and the witness slipped away through the alley. She had done what she came to do—and would live by her decision.

"Family, Tim," Séan said softly, "that's what it's all about. But it doesn't always work out the way you hoped. There's good and bad in everyone."

People came and went, piling more pressure on poor Eily, while her husband sat back at his stool, entertaining his friends and laughing at his own jokes. The two lanky men and the boy left through the front door, the lad still snapping his cap gun like he was in a showdown at the O.K. Corral.

My father and Séan took a slug from their pints and breathed fresh life into their pipes. A silence fell between them. Séan's face clouded, his eyes dull and watery. He took another swallow, a sliver of porter running down his chin.

"'Tis eighteen years since my starry-eyed young fellow took off to fight in France with the Crown against Hitler," he said at last, his voice quivering. He tapped his temple as if to gather the dark thoughts crowding there. His hand shook as he raised the pint.

"A fine young man he was, true enough," my father replied quietly. "You'll never meet the likes of him again."

"Over ten years, we tried for a family. We'd near given up, settled for a life without children. Then he came along, and it changed everything. A reason to get out of bed in the morning. Strong as ten men, chest bursting through his shirt. You should've seen him pike hay or leap for a high ball."

Séan's eyes moistened. He drew a deep, steadying breath.

"He lasted only ten days in Normandy. Then the letter came, saying he had fought bravely and given his life for a great cause.

But let me tell you, that means damn all when you and the missus are left sitting alone by the fire in winter, wondering what might have been. The long nights bring it all back. Sometimes I wish I had woke up dead myself. The only thing that keeps me from cutting loose from this old, rotten world is the thought of what might happen to my Mary. Better dead than alive, we both are, for in truth, while we breathe air through our lungs, we are, in fact, half dead."

My father glanced at the clock. The day was moving on, and we still had business to attend to. One more pint would put paid to that. He held out his glass.

"Here's to the dead, Séan. But I'll have to go before the missus sends out an S.O.S. We'll meet up in the New Year."

Séan slipped me a half crown. "Be good to your mom and dad when you grow up," he said.

"I will, sir," I replied.

I was glad when my father drained the last swallow of porter and we stepped out through the screeching door. It was just as well. Any longer and Séan's melancholy would only have deepened.

Outside, the open fire's flush still burned my cheeks. My lungs, fouled by tobacco and turf smoke, gulped in the cold winter air like a tonic.

My father paused to light his pipe. After a long draw, he said, "I know you heard what Séan had to say. The poor man had it tough. Life isn't always fair, but remember this: there's always someone worse off. It's not what comes your way that matters, but how you deal with it. Life has to go on. Do you understand?"

I didn't, not really. My short life had been sheltered from such hardship. But I nodded anyway. Life has its lessons—the longer you live, the more you learn and in the end life defeats you—no one gets out alive.

Just then, we noticed a robin perched on a low branch, feathers puffed against the chill. We stopped to watch.

"That could be Séan's son, come back to say hello," my father murmured. "They say robins are special that way—they stay close when someone you love has died. Remember that, the next time you miss someone. I know I do."

Walking towards Mannion's shop, I saw a burly Garda take hold of the weedy troublemaker from the pub. He hoisted him by the belt of his trousers and dragged him off towards the barracks. He wouldn't be troubling anyone else that day — and his absence would be missed only for the good.

Passing the gift shop, I craned for another glimpse of the red bicycle. Some lucky fecker would be pedalling it on Christmas morning. I felt a pang of envy before moving on with my father towards Mannion's Fine Tailoring.

But while some found comfort in porter and gossip, others were drawn to smartening themselves up with new clothes — you needed to look the part. The tailor's shop became a place of ceremony, full of measuring tapes, fresh cloth, and quiet pride. If faith began with the rosary, decency began with a new suit — and with luck, it'd last another ten years, provided a man's girth stayed the same.

My Father's Christmas Suit

All of humankind was in the pub that day — the chancers, the lawyers (some would say liars), hardworking Eily and your man — her husband — Sean with his memories, every one of them intact and hard-earned, and my father, holding court over a half pint and a smouldering pipe. The smoke didn't just hang in the air — it infiltrated everything, like a Russian spy in the Cold War. It stung my eyes, clogged my lungs, and wrapped itself around the rafters. The smell of stale porter clung to the walls, mixed with more than the occasional south-westerly gust from someone's nether regions.

The clatter of pint glasses, the scraping of bar stools, the shifting and leaning in, the leaning back again, men slugging pints and downing half-ones, dipping into other people's company uninvited — it was all part of the unspoken curriculum of the local pub. Teaching and learning happened between sips, truth and lies.

Maybe this was education through observation.

It was a relief to get out into the street at last — the sharp air pinching my cheeks and the noise of it all still ringing in my head.

The Christmas display in Mannion's window was a sight to behold — fairy lights twinkled around a tree trimmed with balloons, streamers, and tinsel. A giant

Santa stared out at us, flanked on either side by two impeccably dressed mannequins, each with a look that suggested they'd sooner be in Dublin 4 than stuck in a shopfront in a small town.

The doorbell gave a sharp jangle as we stepped inside. A voice called out from somewhere behind the ranks of neatly hung clothes.

"I'll be with you in two shakes of a lamb's tail. Throw an eye around there while you're waiting, why don't ye? You'd never know what you might find."

We were there that day for one reason and one reason only: for my father's final fitting of his new suit. There was a wedding coming up — up the country — and the old faithful he'd worn to weddings, wakes, and half the Stations in the parish long before he was married was no longer fit for public display. It had seen better days — and plenty of them. Old Methuselah himself would have thought twice about putting it on. Were it not for the camphor balls buried in its pockets, the moths would've eaten it down to the thread.

We made our way towards the source of the voice — and away from the skinning draught that came in every time the door opened. Mannion was kneeling next to some poor man's leg, tape in hand. His marbly eyes peered over glasses that dangled from the tip of his nose. He was a man well past the age of caring what people thought — round face, black oily hair combed back like in the photo of Elvis on the poster outside the cinema.

"Ah, 'tis yourself and the gorsooneen Tim," he said, still crouched. "I'll be with ye now in a minute. The world and its mother is in town today, and I've only the one pair of hands, sadly."

Like the window display outside, the shop inside had a festive feel of its own. Paper chains and tinsel crisscrossed the ceiling like someone had taken a mad notion with a stapler. A small Christmas tree stood on the counter just inside the door, its fairy lights blinking like someone with a bad eye twitch.

The place was long and narrow, with a skylighted ceiling and a U-shaped counter that ran around the walls like a running track. Behind it were doors to small tailoring rooms, each with a little glass window peering out at the main floor — a kind of fashionable confessional. The shelves groaned under the weight of fabric rolls, and here and there you could see where they'd started to bow in the middle.

The floor space was jammed with everything a man from the country might need to make a good impression on someone else, or maybe just on himself: coats, trousers, shirts, shoes, ties, socks, and the odd belt hanging like a forgotten afterthought. It was a proper country shop, in a proper country town, and it felt like it knew its business.

Like everything else in the sixties, life was changing fast. Television had arrived, bringing new ways of thinking. Young people were beginning to question the old certainties — the Church, the State, politics, and the rest. The Showbands were flying high. Cars were a little more plentiful and criss-crossing the county to The Majestic in Mallow, The Hyland in Newmarket, The Arcadia in Cork City, the Lilac Ballroom in Enniskeane — and, occasionally, a raid across the county bounds to the Effin Ballroom in Limerick. The ballrooms were booming, and the hair was getting longer — mostly in protest to the older generation and their ways.

Fashion followed music, and if you wanted to stay in business, you had two choices: adapt or disappear. Or as Bob Dylan put it, the times they are a-changin'.

So it went for Mannion. The old trade of tailoring was slowly going the way of the donkey cart. His made-to-measure suits were being edged out by cheaper, ready-made ones you could grab off a rack and be out the door in five minutes — no tape, no chalk, no ceremony. But Mannion wasn't born yesterday. He kept his ear to the ground and his eye on the small print — mainly the Births, Deaths, and Marriages column in the Cork Examiner.

He knew who had money, who'd lost someone, who was getting hitched, and more importantly, what family they came from. That kind of knowledge was better than any advertising. When someone came through the door looking for a suit or a shirt and tie, Mannion already knew what drawer to open. It was that quiet knowing — and a genuine interest in people — that kept his doors open when plenty of others had folded.

Around the shop, staff climbed up and down stepladders to fetch fabric rolls for curtains or suits.

"Feel the quality of that between your fingers. Here — sure, take a sample swatch home and see what himself thinks of it," an assistant said to an elderly woman.

The woman didn't miss a beat.

"My dear girl, the man I'm married to wouldn't know a bee from a bull's foot about the quality, nor would he care less unless it had four legs and was ready for the mart. It takes all I have in me to get him into town once a year — but the pub, now that's another story. He'd drink porter out of an old sock, so he would.

"So I laid down the law last week. Told him I wouldn't be shamed another minute by the rags he wears. I said he's to invest in a new suit this Christmas, or I'll stop doing his fetching and carrying altogether. And I meant it too.

Those who are bound they must obey, and those who aren't can run away. Take my advice, girleen: stay single if you know what's good for you."

The assistant smiled.

"I will indeed," she said, and carried on with her business.

Closer to where Mannion was attending to his customers, I listened in to the banter.

"Any luck at the old cards this weather, Andy?" he asked from his hunched position, measuring the waist of a very gaunt-looking man.

"Not a bit at all," the man replied.

"The Sweep now — that's a decent win. That's what keeps myself and the missus going. We're always dreaming about what we'd do if we won the Sweep. I'll tell you this, I wouldn't stay here another day, pricking my finger with all these bloody sewing pins."

"You'd miss the hurling and football, though, I'd bet."

"Maybe so. But sure, there's a compromise in everything. We can't have it all. Still, I think I'd side with somewhere sunny — get away from these dreary old winters. Look at the weather out there. My joints are goosed. These old fingers on my hand and the frost outside — they're connected, like night and day. The feckin' arthritis has me nearly crippled."

He paused, then winked at me.

"I'd give the Sweep fong, that's for sure — and to hell with the begrudgers. Isn't that right, young fella?"

My father leaned over and whispered that the man Mannion was talking to was known as Top Sod — because he had a strong pair of hands behind the horse and plough.

Top Sod was now fully engaged.

"To tell you the truth, Dónal," he said, "I never won anything — not even an argument with the missus—and it's just as well, because I'd be tempted to forget about work altogether. The missus always says if I ever won the Sweep, I'd go off the rails completely — gone until the money ran out, and I came back with my tail between my legs."

"Ah now, she's only joking," Mannion replied, out of one side of his mouth — while the other side clamped down on a row of sewing pins. "Sure, Oscar Wilde himself said he could resist everything... except temptation."

"I don't know that Oscar Wilde fella. Is he from around here?" Top Sod asked. "Anyway, if he or any of us won the Sweep, we'd want to watch out — the clergy would find all sorts of charitable causes for the money. Before we knew it, they'd inveigle it out of us quicker than Father Brophy's Mick-the-Miller greyhound could round the track"

He chuckled.

"A tall, good-looking man like yourself, with ample means? Sure, the girls would be swarming," Mannion teased.

"You're a right feckin' caffler altogether, Dónal. There isn't a girl yet born that'd be arsed with the likes of me now. I'll stick with the quare one I have. I think."

"Quare one, is it? Is that all I am to you? I'll show you who's quare!"

That last voice came from a woman standing just behind him — his wife — who he had clearly forgotten was still nearby. Her umbrella landed square across the backs of his legs.

"Out that door, you thundering eejit!"

They both exited the shop, and I quietly wondered if I'd be hearing about murder most foul in the days ahead.

Mannion, unfazed, turned his attention to a stocky man stripped down to shirt and trousers, waiting to be measured for a new coat. A woman stood beside him — likely his wife — and a sulky-faced child was hanging off her arm, cross-legged and full of silent protest.

"What would you do with the Sweep, Denny, if you won it?"

"Oh, be Jaysus, I'd give it fong too, Donal," said Denny. "My winnings wouldn't be going to put silver on the parish priest's sideboard, I'll tell you that. I have my own worthy causes — and plenty of 'em."

"God save your blasted soul, Denny Cronin. The parish priest is only doing his duty, the poor man."

"As sure as there's piss in a puck, he won't see a farthing of my money — not while I'm the boss of my own house."

"I often wonder what I'm doing living in the same house," the woman muttered, making the sign of the cross and rolling her eyes to Heaven.

"I might be after starting World War Three here," Mannion whispered to my father from the corner of his mouth.

I guessed from their conversations that the parish priest was not the most popular behind closed doors.

Mannion stood up slowly, stretching his back.

"That's it now — we're done, Denny. I'll have it ready for you on the twentieth and not a day sooner. And don't leave it till the last minute to collect it."

Mannion looped the tape measure around his neck once more, and Denny, his wife, and the pouty-faced child exited to the sound of the doorbell jingling behind them.

The shop was buzzing, full of elbows, hangers, and flustered conversations — but then a voice rose above the din.

It came from a teenager near the coat rack — a lanky streak of misery, all sneer and Brylcream, arms folded like he was holding up the wall. He was trying to be a Teddy Boy — the same way Paddy from the village fancied himself one, with his winkle pickers, drainpipe trousers, and hair sculpted into a quiff at the front and a duck's arse at the back. Paddy used to wear sunglasses even when the sky was full of grey clouds. He'd prop himself against the corner wall of the shop, angled for a ninety-degree view both ways — front and rear — and he'd glare at passers-by like a man after reading James Dean's autobiography twice and believing every word of it. The Sullivan twins lived in mortal fear of him. Every Sunday, on their way to Mass, they'd round the corner at a gallop and bless themselves for protection.

In fairness, Paddy's menace was mostly performance. But the lad in the shop today — he had the costume, the stance, and the same notion of danger… minus the mystique.

His mother was at the end of her tether, flinging trousers and jackets at him like she was lobbing grenades.

"Try these on and stop making a holy show of me."

"I will not. I'm not wearing that! It looks like something Father Brophy would wear to a funeral."

"Well, at least he wears trousers that fit! You look like you were poured into yours and forgot to say when."

"Try that on," she snapped, shoving a hanger into his chest. "My patience is wearing thin. I'm warning you — your father'll take skelps out of you if you go home still wearing that… well, whatever the Hell you call it."

"He couldn't care less. He's always saying I should express myself more. Stand up for myself more."

"Express yourself, is it? Well, let me express myself for a minute. You'll try that on or you'll find yourself on the express train with a one-way ticket to your uncle in the city. He'll knock the tasby out of you — straighten you out, you useless, good-for-nothing bostoon."

"It's fashion, mother. God, you haven't a clue. Rory Gallagher wears stuff like this."

"Rory Gallagher? You can barely play the tin whistle. Now stop your old RíRá and put them on before I lose the rag completely."

"I'm serious. After Christmas, I'm gone—I'm making my own way in the world."

"Own way. You couldn't work your way out of a paper bag. The only thing you've made in this world is a nuisance of yourself."

"I'm not ending up like Uncle Roger, anyway—stinking of coal dust and sweat, faking a bad back for money."

"How dare you say that about your Uncle Roger! He's one of the hardest-working men walking. That man's done more honest work before breakfast than you'll manage in a year of staring at yourself in the mirror. He works the docks in Cork — back-breaking stuff, loading coal boats — comes home black as turf and still finds time to use his head."

When the old back acts up from the job, he's well entitled to what's due. He uses his head — and his connections, that's all. Your cousin in Glanmire works in the insurance office, and a straighter man never walked. If Roger was claiming anything crooked, he'd be the first to say no. It's all above board — not like those solicitors, who wouldn't dirty their hands with honest work but have no bother making money off men like your Uncle Roger."

"He's a chancer. 'Tis funny how he always seems to have a bad back during the year and loads of money for drink around Christmas."

"A chancer, is it? I'll give you chancer, you dickeryda. Shut your gob before you shame the whole family. Your uncle works hard! You'd be lucky to have half his gumption. All your Brylcreem and posing — not a bubble between your ears. Rory Gallagher, my foot. You're more like Rory O'Back-of-the-Class, daydreaming your way to stardom. There'll be no stardom with that carry-on, I'll tell you something for nothing."

With that, she gave him a sharp smack across the back of the legs with a wooden coat hanger.

"Ow! Jaysus, will you stop that!"

He turned and caught me looking.

"What are you looking at?" he snapped, flashing the two fingers.

I tried to duck my head — and misjudged it completely, cracking it off the coat rail behind me.

"Stupid Teddy clown," I muttered, rubbing the sore spot.

His mother saw what happened.

"Take no notice of him, boyeen. He's only brave when he's got Brylcream and an audience. Behind them, stupid glasses is the biggest softie ever on two legs."

The Teddy bolted from the shop, his mother right on his heels.

"You get that old streak from your father's brother — odd as two left feet, God rest him — notions of Bing Crosby, the voice of a crow, and the manners of a pig in a parlour. And another thing—"

But the shop door slammed behind them before we could hear what else she had to say.

I wasn't too bothered about what'd become of him when he got home.

At last, Mannion arrived to attend to my father, who stood there stiffly, arms half-raised, wearing the old suit he'd sworn still had "plenty of life in it." The elbow was as shiny as a wet stone, and the cuffs were fraying.

Mannion stepped in with a mock-up coat.

"Right, Tim — arms out there like you're a scarecrow in the middle of a field."

My father grumbled but stuck out his arms anyway.

"I don't know why we need a new one at all. This one is grand for any wedding, or for wakes and funerals—
Come to think of it, it's much the same thing."

He glanced down at the white chalk marks tracing his torso.

"God help us… I look like a lined hurling pitch."

Mannion stepped back and squinted.

"You do… but more like a lamb-raddled one on the side of a mountain.
Don't worry — I only cut my cloth according to your measure unless you're after putting on too much condition.
You'll be the swankiest man at any wedding for the next ten years."

"God, Tim — how many have you now? Six, is it? Sure, you nearly have your own hurling team: all fine, strong lads, the lot of them. I suppose you'll hurl for Cork yet," he said, turning to me.

"I doubt it," I replied shyly.

"Plenty of time yet, plenty of time yet! Isn't that right, Tim?"

"The man that made time made plenty of it," my father said, beginning to loosen his arms.

"That'll do for now," Mannion nodded. "I'll have it ready for you on the twentieth. And whatever you do, don't leave it till Christmas Eve — or I might be on the missing list. I've a long-standing appointment every Christmas Eve with a few chaps by the name of John Jameson and his cousin Arthur Guinness."

Our business done, we stepped back out into the street. The frosty air bit at my cheeks as we crossed to the footpath. Across the road, the Teddy Boy and his mother were still at it — the same row rumbling on, as if nothing in the world had moved since we went in.

If the tailor's shop was a man's domain, the real trial came when a young lad found himself dragged into the ladies' drapery. There he'd stand, red-faced among bolts of satin and boxes of doodankies, praying none of his school pals would walk by. Between the measuring and the mortification, it was enough to make a fella wish the floor would open. And when the trousers finally arrived, there was so much room in them you could nearly hatch a goose — as they said, and often did.

No Place to Hatch a Goose

My father and I met up with my mother at the top of Strand Street. My brother was sticking close to her, and guess what, wasn't he only holding a cap gun in his hand and threatening to shoot half the pedestrians who made eye contact with him? I wondered if I had made a mistake tagging along with my father earlier; there was no chance, not even a hint of a cap gun, for me in the company I was keeping.

But, on the other hand, I did have Séan's half-crown in my pocket, which might buy me a lucky bag or, God forbid, a few more Gobstoppers.

Anyway, I gave up on my father and deserted to my mother's side, where I might have a better chance of getting a pre-festive present out of the blue from her. My mother was like that — generous and kind. However, it wasn't long before I regretted my decision. She stopped outside Tracy's Ladies' Shop and said:

'I must go in here for a minute to get a few doodankies.'

Doodankies. The word sounded strange. What in the name of— bless me father for I have sinned, are doodankies. I had no idea, but it didn't matter. What I *did* know was that a lady's shop was no place for a young fellow to be seen in. Imagine the shame — shopping with my mother for mysterious doodankies, surrounded by women, frills, and chatter. I could never show my face outside the house again.

I protested, but my mother shot me down with a reminder:

'Your brother never gave me one bit of trouble.'

'Of course he didn't', I thought to myself, "isn't he the cute boy?"

And that was why he now had a cap gun in his hand to kill half the town. I must admit, it was hard to argue with that.

Resigned to my fate, I followed in after her. The place was no bigger than a Dorney's small goat shed— tight enough with five or six inside, and tighter still when three of them were carrying a few extra pounds, not in their purses, you know what I mean—I'll say no more.

Packed to the rafters it was, with balls of wool, corset boxes, underthings, and every manner of female luxury.

The women were deep in their talk — not a one of them in any rush to finish what they'd come in for. You'd swear Mrs Tracy was paying them by the hour to block out the cold — and fair play, they were earning it. Not a breath of fresh air to be had.

My mother spotted a woman she knew, Madge, and the two of them launched into a conversation that took them across the Atlantic and back, as if they had all the time in the world.

I, meanwhile, was wedged between a button stand and the broad backsides of two chattering women, deep in debate with Mrs Tracy over the finer points of flannel knickers. One sudden shove from either of those posteriors and the whole stand would come crashing down — with me caught in the wreckage.

Luckily, they stood their ground, and the stand stayed where it was.

Unfortunately, things took a turn for the worse. One of the women let off a silent but deadly fart, drifting southward — and with me standing level with her rear end, I caught the full, eye-watering blast.

Whatever she'd eaten, the smell rose around me like a gluggar — like someone had just coughed up eggs they ate last Easter. I swear I lost part of my childhood in that moment — and I've never fully got it back.

In the height of my suffocation, all I could think of was the beautiful sulphurous smell of my brother's cap gun — and him out there, shooting half the town and getting off scot-free.

Mrs Tracy was a pleasant-enough woman in her middle years, with ginger hair that had gone a bit to straw, and a freckled face that spoke of summers long since spent in a hayfield. She presided over the chaos with the calm of a woman well used to it — and truth be told, she seemed to relish it.

She moved between the customers with the ease of a priest receiving a few bob at the October stations — full of small talk and sly observations.

'Feel the flannel on them knickers now, missus. They're double-gusseted — elastic top and bottom with no end of comfort, no matter which way you twist or turn. And I'll tell you this much — himself will be dying to get his hands on you.'

That she said with a wink to a worn-looking woman half-sunk behind two full shopping bags straining all the way to the floor.

The woman gave a high-pitched chuckle.

'Ah, I think I'll leave it for today. I'll keep a tight hold on the ones I have. Can't you see the state of me? The last thing I need is himself getting ideas — and me pacing the cold lino at three in the morning while he's snoring away without a care. No, thank you kindly.'

She turned to go, and on the spin swung her handbag like a hurley — and caught me square in the ear. I stumbled, but recovered, and thanked God she was going. I'd more room to breathe at last.

I glanced at my mother — still locked in conversation with Madge, who was holding up a pair of knickers like you would a forensic exhibit in a court of law.

'Sure, these feckin' yokes would fit Tadgh na Goolta himself! You don't think I'm that size, surely, do you, Mrs Tracy?'

'Ah, no, Madge — I'm just a bit flustered. I must've handed you the wrong pair. I'm sorry — it's been one of those days,' Mrs Tracy replied, doing her best to stay diplomatic.

But Madge wasn't letting it go.

'You could hatch a goose in the arse of them knickers — they're so feckin' big!'

Mrs Tracy said no more. After all, the least said is soonest mended. Head down, she rooted through another box of doodankies until — at last — she unearthed the right size.

I couldn't tell if Madge was happy or mad, the way she stormed off, still muttering something about Tadgh na Goolta and a goose.

Maybe they were for him—Tadgh—ah no, perish the thought, for God's sake.

Just after Madge left, the door opened again, and in stepped a starchy-looking woman with a powdered face and the air of an Irish wolfhound with its head held high — proud and showing the world who was boss.

'Would you mind if I skipped ahead?' she asked my mother. 'I've a sick mother-in-law waiting for her dinner — and she's not a wan to be crossed.'

There's two of ye now, I thought.

My mother, ever the peacemaker, gave a tired smile and nodded — though she cast her eyes to Heaven in silent appeal.

The woman began examining a corset so fearsome it looked like it had seen military service. With all the steel and strapping in it, you'd swear it could hold back a stampede of bulls — or tow a German tank out of Nadd bog.

'Um… I don't know… maybe… maybe not… we'll see…' she muttered, pawing at it like it was a bomb she wasn't sure about defusing.

And all I could think was: *Will you, for God's sake, make up your mind so I can get out of here?*

After what felt like a fortnight, she sighed and relented.

'Ah, sure, I'll take it. There's no hold in the one I have anyway… go on before I change my mind.'

Mrs Tracy didn't give her the chance. She had it wrapped, bagged, and the woman out the door in a flash.

Thank God for small mercies.

Eventually, it was my mother's turn to be served. It took only a few minutes.

Pity, I thought, *she wasn't a bit more like the starchy woman who just left the shop — I'd have been out of the henhouse long ago and maybe dodged the gluggar.*

I'll never know. Then again, my suffering might've been far worse if the starchy woman *was* my mother.

Anyway, before you could say *Hould your whist*, she'd bought a few pairs of thick winter socks for my father and a pair of kid gloves for herself for Sunday Mass — in and out without a fuss.

As we left the shop, I promised myself it was the last time Mrs Tracy would ever see or hear from me. I'd never again be caught going where no man should ever go. Strange new worlds would have to do without me.

A few doors down the street, we stopped at Hawe's Gift Shop. The display window was the real cat's pyjamas; train sets, toy tractors and — in the centre — the object of my dreams: the red-and-white bicycle with gleaming white tyres.

I had never dared ask my parents for it, knowing it would never be mine. I'd told Santa. Every night, kneeling by my bed, I whispered my wish to him — not *Him*, though trusting Santa more than God was probably a mistake.

'Don't stir from there,' my mother said as she stepped inside, leaving me outside to admire the display.

My heart raced. Could this be it? Was she buying me the bicycle? Feck the cap gun — the bike was the real business.

I peeked through the window and saw Mrs Hawe writing something on a piece of paper. A receipt, perhaps? My hopes soared, only to be dashed as my mother turned to leave.

'I'll pop by in the New Year, Biddy, and we'll have a proper chat,' she said. 'You can tell me all about the goings-on with Ned Roche and the floozy from Galtymore.'

With that, she walked off, and I knew well there'd be no bike for me — not unless the man from the North Pole had a sudden attack of conscience and decided to stop discriminating against the likes of us.

I could see it plain as day: the boy with the velvet-collared coat, lording it up on my red bicycle come Christmas morning, while his mother looked out from behind the lace curtains, all pride and polish, and poor Ruby sweating in the kitchen over their dinner.

Ah, indeed — the haves and the have-nots.

And sure wasn't it the very same in Communist Russia under Nikita Khrushchev — only with less tinsel and more turnips?

The darkness closed in as we made our way for the spin home. We passed the pub where my father stood talking to Seán and another man. Seán was by now unsteady on his feet; he pressed a shilling into my hand, and I thought how grand it would be to meet him more often, except not in the pub.

Over the bridge, we ran into the same woman from that morning, still dragging her tantrum-throwing child behind her.

"But you promised — you did — I still want it! I'll be good!" the little pain-in-the-arse wailed, clutching a doll with its legs sticking out of a bag.

"When we get home," the mother said through gritted teeth, "it's straight to bed for you. But not before you get a proper hiding from your father. Come on, you impudent pup — you've shamed me enough for one day."

I thought to myself — tis the likes of that little wagon that'll get my grand red and white bike. What she should've got was a good, solid kick up the arse.

The drive home was quiet — just the low hum of the engine, the occasional grind of gears from Uncle Liam's car, and the stop-start rhythm of conversation between him and my father. Wrapped up in my own world, it never dawned on me what Liam had gotten up to for the day.

My mother seemed content — grateful not to be making memories like the year before and the pony-and-trap episode. Some things are better remembered by their absence.

The exhaustion lay heavy on all of us until silence settled over the car like a blanket.

I stared out the window, my mind replaying the day's misadventures — the pub, the embarrassment in Tracy's shop, the red-and-white bike that would never be mine, and that annoying little pain-in-the-you-know-where child.

When we reached home, my mother fired up the range, set the cast-iron kettle hissing, and brewed a grand pot of tea. My father sank into his armchair with a satisfied sigh. My brother, still armed to the teeth, marched around the kitchen with his cap gun, shooting imaginary villains. He yapped on about his cap gun adventures — blissfully unaware of the close-quarters combat I'd endured with flannel knickers and goose-sized undergarments… or the heartbreak I'd swallowed outside Hawe's window.

I sat at the table, eating a slice of Binchy's curny cake and sipping a warming cup of tea — and I realised that these were the small moments that made Christmas magic.

Around Christmas time, the postman, was half-saint, half-saviour— bringing word from sons, daughters cousins. A knock on the door could bring joy or sorrow, but it always brought life. The whole parish seemed to hold its breath, waiting for his step on the gravel.

The Christmas Post

Danny the postman had no grá for Christmas. To him, it was four weeks of torture, a month-long penance served on two wheels with a bulging sack on his back and no thanks at the end of it. He said it every year: "There's more people writing lies in them cards than ever told the truth in confession."

Come December, the whole parish went stone mad. People who hadn't licked a stamp since the foundation of the State were suddenly buying envelopes and Christmas cards as if there was no tomorrow, and sometimes only sending them a few hundred yards up the road to their neighbours.. "They'd be quicker walking to the house themselves," he'd mutter to himself as he rummaged through his postbag. Sure, he knew all their handwriting, the small squinty writing—that was Tady Murphy's, the big floury flourish –that was Maureen O'Donnell writing for Mick the Football. 'Love from all of us, twould say," from people who hadn't spoken to each other all year.

Danny was, shall we say, long in the tooth and past the age where any sane man should be straddling the high-bar pushbike with a sack full of letters and cards, but the postmaster hadn't the nerve to tell him. The years of dragging himself out of bed in the pitch-black, with a wonky hip and knees not much better, were catching up fast. He'd curse the cold as he pulled on his stiff trousers, muttering dark curses about the Department of Posts and Telegraphs and the crowd in Head Office who never once cycled up a country boreen in their lives.

Still, out he went — every blessed morning — rain, hail, or sleet, to sort the post and saddle up like a man heading to the gallows.

The round would kill a horse—more hills than ancient Rome, and every one steeper than the last. Danny peddled up and down country lanes so narrow the birds had to jump sideways out of the hedge to avoid him — and half the time they didn't, they just launched themselves at his face for sport.

The boreens were a disgrace: craters big enough to swallow a horse and plough, and not a trace of a council worker since Dev was in short pants. And to crown it all, there was always some half-mad mongrel lying in wait behind a gate, eyes full of murder and teeth sharp as daggers. Danny'd pedal like the devil was after him, roaring curses back over his shoulder that'd curl the hair on a poodle.

One time, a dog sank its teeth into the front tyre and punctured it clean through. Danny had to either requisition a new one — which meant paperwork, signatures, delays — or cannibalise an old wreck of a bike from behind the shed. Naturally, he did the latter. The crowd in Head Office were more concerned with ink stamps and filing cabinets than getting a letter to a woman who might be waiting on word from her son in England or America— or better still, a few folded pounds or dollars tucked inside.

There were times he'd skid on a sheet of ice, land hard on his arse, and end up tangled in the bike frame like hay in a skeater.

To be fair, there wasn't a bit of drama on him. He'd haul himself up, check that nothing was broken, curse the ice, and carry on.

Keeping your head and maintaining your dignity — that was part of the job.

Speaking of which — on wet mornings, and there were plenty of them, he wore the full get-up: a black cape much the same as the parish priest's, only less costly, flapping from the handlebars, covering man and mailbag alike. Bulging yellow oilskins around the legs, shiny with boreen muck, and goloshes like a sheep farmer out of Priest's Leap, down Bantry way.

His regulation peaked cap — XL, by the look of it, sat low over the eyes and ears like an FCA helmet.

He looked like a cross between a bishop, a mountainey man, and a crow travelling against the wind— but by God, he always delivered the post without fail.

Danny was, on the face of it, an ordinary man. But if there was one thing he adored more than a tame dog and a dry boreen, it was digging into the tangled roots of local family trees. And by God were they tangled, half the crowd on this side of the parish never fished beyond their local river. One way or another, everyone was related to each other, and Danny knew all their history, the ones who had married badly, and the ones who should never have married at all.

"What Danny didn't know about the parish," people would say, "wasn't worth knowing."

Others weren't so generous. "He goes out of his way," said one man, "to unearth things that were buried for good reason."

"Let sleeping dogs lie," said another.

"Ah," said Danny, "but I've a habit of waking the right ones."

In the days before apps, dating sites, and all that auld carry-on, matchmaking was still alive and kicking — especially for those who'd left it a bit late putting their name on the racecard. The cuckoo clock was ticking louder by the year, and in danger of shutting up altogether.

Now, the matchmaker might arrange the introductions — that was their trade — but it was Danny who could tell you the stuff that mattered: the Dúchas.

And you know what they say about the Dúchas?

Well, if you don't, I'll tell you — *Briseann an dúchas trí shúile an chait.*- Nature breaks out through the eyes of a cat.

And that's just the start of it. The bloodlines, the drink habits, the land holdings, the secret cousins in Mallow, which side they took in the Civil War — and most of all, *why*.

I know a man who ate the ear off a sheep — while it was still alive — out of pure spite.

Danny would conduct a thorough background check on the intended — not out of malice, no — but because, in his view, marriage was a lifelong commitment and a potentially harmful investment at that.

"One look before," he'd say, "is always better than two after," or "let the dog see the rabbit," whatever in God's name that meant.

By mid-December, Danny'd be up to his eyeballs — working Saturdays, Sundays too if he could swing it, for the double time, or was it time and a half — trying to stay ahead of the flood of cards, parcels, and general Christmas desperation.

Now, I had no interest in the post at all — not until Christmas. And only then because there was a half-decent chance something might actually be addressed to me.

The rest of the year, it was nothing but bills, brown envelopes, no, not what you're thinking, and long-winded moans from cousins in far-flung corners of the country.

But come December, hope sprang up like the Rahilly twins — long strings of misery, the two of them.

So I'd be at the front gate early, hand out like the collection box at Sunday mass, waiting for Danny to jaunt up the hill with his sack and his cronawning.

And when he handed me the bundle of cards — and there *was* a bundle, same time every year, like a holy

Christian ritual — I'd carry it the final few yards to the kitchen table like an altar boy bringing the wine to the priest at Mass.

Opening those cards was a ritual, too.

The names, the messages, the fountain pen blobs, the crossed nibs that scratched the paper, the faded glitter — I read them all like they were telegrams from the Christy Ring himself.

One time, we got someone else's post by mistake — I declare to God it was a holy terror what was in it.

Wasn't it for Pat Joe Houlihan from back Carty's Bridge way, and wasn't it summoning him to court over an unlicensed bull?

We didn't know what to do with it, so we did nothing — only threw it in the fire.

And sure, Houlihan was a decent old sort.

No point ruining his Christmas over a Fresian Bull.

Best of all, Aunt Nonie — my silver-haired godmother, with a hairy chin and a rasper of a tongue — sent me a box of chocolates every Christmas without fail.

Same brand. Two layers. Dairy Milk, back when there was more than a glass and a half in every chocolate.

Same brown paper. Same rectangle shape. Tied with twine, waxed over like a legal document in case of any interference.

You could set your watch by it.

The Saturday before Christmas was a right hoor of a day — rain pelting down sideways, streaming outside our gate and lodging like a pond in Uncle Tom's field. My brother and I were crouched under the chestnut tree in the front garden, coats over our heads, half-drowned and pretending we weren't cold.

Then we saw him — Danny, head down, arse back, soldiering up the hill like Napoleon retreating from Waterloo. We bolted for the porch like Fly, our greyhound, first out of the trap.

"Morning, gentlemen," he called, his voice half-drowned in the deluge of rain that was sheeting off him and running down his cheeks and off his cape like gutter water from the cow stall. He leaned his bike inside the porch, where the smell of wet wool was worse than sheep on sheep-dipping day.

Rex, our sheepdog, came skidding around the corner and tried to nose his way inside — nearly toppling Danny's bike in the process.

"Get out, ya dirty mongrel!" my brother roared, landing a boot on Rex's rear and sending him yelping back into the downpour.

Danny just chuckled. "What's Santa bringing ye for Christmas, boys?"

"A toy soldier, a drum, and a kick in the bum," said my brother.

"Well," Danny grinned, "he might bring you nothing with a gob like that."

Then he squinted down at the envelopes — with one eye pointing to Cork and the other to Kerry, like they were after arguing over the disallowed goal in the Munster final.

"Have I a Master Maurice here? Because I've something for him."

Have I a master Maurice, my eye, and he knowing well who I was and everyone belonging to me.

"I'm him," I said anyway, chest out like I was being called to fight for my country.

"You're popular today," he said, handing over three large cards. "Fine big ones, too — and not a bill among them."

"That's all?" I said, disappointed.

Danny ignored me and turned to my brother. "And you must be Master Billy — three for you too, you cheeky article. And here's another handful for the house."

I was halfway to the door, already picturing the kitchen table and the ripping of envelopes, when Danny called me back.

"Hold on, Master Maurice — I'm not done with you yet."

From the front carrier, he produced a rectangular parcel, wrapped exactly like the year before, and the year before that again.

"For you," he said.

I took the parcel with the manners my mother taught me — and with greed too— sure who would blame me— my heart thumping like the hammers of Hell. It was addressed to *Master Maurice* in royal blue fountain pen ink and sealed, as I said.

I gave it a quick rattle. Yes, I knew that sound —the soft thud of the chocolates shifting tightly and dying to be left loose.

"Merry Christmas!" Danny called, mounting his bike with a creak from the chain. Off he pedalled up the hill to the cranky neighbours.

I bolted into the kitchen, nearly took the door off the hinges, tore off the brown paper, and there it was — a proper box of chocolates. Tucked inside was a note in Aunt Nonie's slanted hand — my silver-haired godmother, the cratereen with the hairy chin and the voice like a crow with the flu.

To My Godchild Maurice,
Have a lovely Christmas and behave so Santa will bring you something nice.
Be sure to share the sweets with your mother and father and your brothers.
From your loving Godmother,
Aunt Nonie.

Before anyone could read it, I shoved the note into my pocket and burned it in the range at the first opportunity. To be fair, I did offer one sweet each to everyone — after I'd picked out the best ones for myself, naturally.
I devoured the rest, savouring each bite.

But sweet divine Jesus, they tasted like Christmas — rich, fleeting, and like my youth itself — gone too soon.

Not every Christmas made the papers, though. Some were quiet affairs — whispered over tea, half-forgotten by everyone but those who lived them. The kind of stories that start with, "You'll hardly remember, but..." and end with a sigh. They never made the headlines, yet they stay with you longer than the rest. Every family has one. This next is ours.

There was another Christmas - Shhh!

Poor old Danny fell sick one Christmas — a proper collapse, the kind that sets the neighbours whispering rosaries and laying bets. Flat on his back for three solid days, they were on the verge of sending for the priest to anoint him. Touch and go, by all accounts. You'd swear he'd been poisoned, but it was only the flu — with a splash of pneumonia for good measure.

The whole parish was in a flap. What would happen to the letters and cards — especially the ones with something folded inside? You could find a hen with a mouthful of teeth easier than a postman that week.

Christmas was always chaos at the Post Office. People who hadn't posted a letter all year were suddenly scribbling cards to cousins in Cricklewood, Mullingar, Newbridge, Drom and Dromina, Ardglass, America and anywhere else that could claim a relation. And it wasn't just the outgoing post — no, no, it was the incoming, the important stuff that had the place crippled, envelopes thick with news or thin with a pound or even a ten shilling note—all donations welcome. Parcels arriving from

America with the speed of divine intervention and totally useless. Some indeed did have a few pounds or dollars tucked inside, and fair play to them for that, but the rest of it? Christ above, what were they thinking? Now, don't get me wrong, the gesture was appreciated. The parcels from Uncle Sam! Sweet Divine Jaysus. I ask you: what good was a baseball bat in a town where no one had a clue what baseball even was? We didn't have burglars. If anything, we were all trying to sneak out, not the burglars breaking in.

Another time, we got a pair of jodhpurs — jodhpurs, I swear to God — no one knew what they were. The neighbours came round for a viewing like it was a holy relic. We thought it might be some sort of Protestant underpants.

Then there were the fancy neckties. A full box of them arrived one year — so shiny you'd nearly need sunglasses to look at them. No self-respecting man would wear one to Mass, or anywhere else, either. My mother eventually sewed them into a patchwork quilt to spare them the shame of being seen.

Anyway, the post office was bursting. And if someone didn't step up soon, there'd be blood spilled on the counter before the turkey hit the oven.

That's when someone — and no one ever admitted who — came up with the inspired but disastrous idea of calling Richie McNeill.

Now, Richie hadn't carried a postbag in fifteen years, and what he lacked in fitness, he made up for in a passionate, long-standing relationship with the drink. He was more familiar with the snug in Alley Bar than the front step of a rural cottage. If you went looking for a worse candidate, you'd have to consult Father Mathew himself — and even he'd struggle to name a man with hollower legs. Sure, Richie would drink whiskey out of a dirty sock — then ask for a straw.

It was said — and not always in jest — that Richie was the only man in the parish who could make the mad mongrel retreat to the haybarn when he arrived. Some even claimed the poor dog was trying to sign up as a Pioneer in self-defence.

Christmas Eve arrived in a squall of sleet and last-minute panic. Inside our house, the Stanley range was blazing, my mother knee-deep in stuffing the turkey — a fine big black one, twenty-one pounds — and 'twouldn't last long either in a house like ours, if you knew the place. My father was scanning the Old Moore's Almanac to see what the future held, and of course, the Holly Bough and the quizzes and the kind of Christmasses the city crowd had back in the day. The only thing missing was the post.

“Where in God’s name is he?” my mother muttered, wiping her hands on her apron. “He should’ve been here hours ago.” She was anxious to hear from her sister in Youghal, gone down with a bad dose of pleurisy, and if you were depending on her useless bunch of children or her red-nosed husband to inform you of her well-being, you’d be waiting. The most useless crowd God ever put on this earth.

Just then, poor old Rex started yowling at the gate — another oddity if ever I saw one — never learned how to bark proper — yowling like the devil himself had appeared in a pair of goloshes.

My father looked up. “Listen, there’s a car on the bridge.” He used to say that even though the nearest bridge was five miles away — God bless his hearing.

I was sent out to investigate, and what I found at the gate stopped me in my tracks.

There, sprawled on the frozen ground like a scarecrow after a storm, was the bould Richie Roche — arms flung wide, postbag half-open, bicycle laid out like a spider’s web and Richie’s feet tangled in the frame. The whiff of drink off him was enough to revive an elephant or send a smaller one to its grave.

"Get off me, for feck’s sake, youngfella!" came the roar from the depths of the heap.

Between my brother and me, we dragged him inside, deadweight like he was a pig after the slaughter. My mother, half-shocked, shoved a mug of strong tea in front of him. Richie blinked at the light like a man seeing angels.

"Hollow legs, he should be called, a pure martyr for the drink," she muttered.

"If he's a martyr, he'll set Hell ablaze, that's if it's down he's going," said my father, dry as ever.

Richie tried to straighten up in the kitchen chair, but managed only a slow lean to the left. He accepted the tea like it was the Holy Communion.

"Ye're good people," he murmured, blinking again. "I always said it. Not like them... them... crowd above... stealing m'buttons…"

"Jaysus, he's flutered," Jackie laughed out loud.

"Who's stealing your buttons, Richie?" I asked, trying not to laugh, myself.

He looked at me sideways, suspicious. "The post... the postbags, boy. The bags know. They whisper at night, y'know. They know who's drinkin'... and who's not. Tell 'em, tell 'em I said it."

Jackie leaned in, serious as a judge. "We'll pass that on to the Minister for Post and Telegraphs."

Richie squinted. "Minister for... for tea, teetotalers, is it? 'Cause I've a bone to pick with that old hoor too."

We could barely contain ourselves.

"Richie," said Billy, straight-faced, "try saying Merry Christmas backwards?"

Richie's eyes rolled. "Sss… Ssshmerry Crissbus…"

We fell around the place laughing.

"Crissbus!" Jackie roared. "He's after inventing a new feast day!"

"Saint Richie, the Scuttered!" I piped in.

Richie raised a finger to make a point, dripped tea down his shirt, and muttered, "That's... tha's lib-libullus... libby... lib... Shut up, ye little savages."

The only thing upright about Richie that Christmas Eve was the bicycle — and even that was bent sideways from the fall.

While the mother and father were fussing, we started rooting through Richie's postbag like it was Christmas morning. Jackie found a damp envelope and gave it a sniff. A whiff of Old Spice aftershave came off it like 'twould kill a ferret.

"Miss Hannah Nora Grainger! Who's writing to her? She's as sour as Seanie Hanrahan's milk on a hot July day."

Jackie opened it. We'd no shame.

He read aloud, spitting out every second word:

"*Dearest Hannah Nora, my one true rosebud.*

I hope this finds you well and not too frozen in the cold weather."

We howled.

"I wanted to write to you before Christmas, because I know you get very down this time of year, what with the talk and the pressure from the likes of your wan with the notions. Let me say again, and I mean it now: you're the one for me."

It was hard to contain ourselves. We all started skitting, and Jackie blurted tea down his nose.

"I know it's been twenty years, but sure the Lord hasn't taken my mother yet. She's hanging on. Her health isn't what it was, and I know what you're going to say – that it wasn't what it was fifteen years ago either, when we first spoke about tying the knot. But, she can only come back from the dead so many times. But once she pops her clogs — and God forgive me for saying it — we'll be free to make our plans. Maybe next year or the year after will be our year — or at least the one after that. Surely..."

"What kind of an old eejit is that fella?" my mother accidentally let slip and made a faint-hearted attempt to grab the letter.

Jackie kept going, holding the letter up close.

"So don't go bothering yourself about that quare one from the post office social. God forbid I'd be talking like that, but there's no future in it — not with her knees and her attitude.

We were howling like Rex now. Or was it yowling?

"And Hannah — keep the wishbone from your Christmas Goose for me. We'll pull it together in the New Year, and may the longer half be mine if you're still waiting.

Forever yours, today, tomorrow and always.

Your loving sweetheart, Dinny Joe."

My mother snatched it back with a smile and tossed it into the bag as if it were a mortal sin.

"God help poor Hannah," she said and left it at that, even though I knew there was more to it than in the letter about Dinny Joe's mother.

With a lot of grunting and groaning, we finally got Richie back out on the road. His tie was sideways, his cap pulled down over one ear, tea stains on his shirt. Watching him mount the bike was like watching a dog trying to climb a gate. We nearly died laughing as he wobbled down the road.

A week later, a farmer found the postbag in a ditch, half the letters soggy, the rest nibbled by rats or something else you wouldn't want to think about. The farmer and his wife dried them out by the fire and read every one. Miss Grainger's letter had the ink run clean off it. All that was left was"

"*Your loving sweeheart, Dinny Joe."*

Complaints flew in. Accusations too. Lost cards, misdelivered parcels, and talk of criminal interference and civil proceedings.

Richie was hauled into the postmaster's office for a termination interview. He tried to speak for himself, but it was hard to take him seriously with brandy on his breath and a Christmas pudding stain on his trousers.

And that was the end of Richie Roche's brief and blotchy comeback.

Every year since, when the post lands on the mat and someone moans that Danny's handwriting was neater, someone else pipes up: "Ah, but do you remember the Christmas of poor Richie Roche?" And the laughter starts all over again..

But silence never lasted long in our part of the world. Once the secret sorrows were folded away, the noise came roaring back — feathers, laughter, and a chorus of gobbles loud enough to drown out regret. The season was rolling on again, with turkeys to kill, prayers to say, and time running short for both.

Turkey's Say Your Prayers

Now, before we get to our own misadventures, spare a thought for the turkey — for if anyone dreads Christmas, it's him.

When I was a young turkey,
new to the house,
My little big brother whispered; be quiet as a mouse,
He stuttered and stammered and stammered and stuttered,
But soon, I knew just what he muttered,
His look and his tone I will always remember,
When he told me of the horrors of ... Black November;
'Come about August, now listen to me,
Each day you'll get fat, you'll no longer be thin,
And grow a big rubbery thing under your chin.
'And then one morning, when you're warm in your bed,
The farmer's wife will burst in and hack off your head,'
'She'll pluck out your feathers, till you're bald and pink,
then scoop out your insides and leave you lying in the sink

'And then comes the worst part,' he said without bluffing,
'She'll spread your cheeks and pack your rear with stuffing. '
Well, the rest of his words were too grim to repeat,
I sat on the porch like a winged piece of meat,
And decided on the spot that to avoid being cooked,
I'd have to lay low and remain overlooked;
I began a new diet of nuts and granola,
High-roughage salads, juice and diet cola,
And as they ate pastries, chocolates and crepes,
I stayed in my room doing Jane Fonda steps,

I maintained my weight of two pounds and a half,
And tried not to notice when the bigger birds laughed;
But 'twas I who was laughing, under my breath,
As they chomped and they chewed, ever closer to death;

And sure enough, when Black November rolled around,
I was the last turkey left, not worth being found,
So now I'm a pet, in the farmer's wife's lap;
I haven't a worry, so I eat, and I nap,
She held me today, while sewing and humming,
Then smiled at me and said, "Christmas is coming........"

Black November – A Turkey's Lament Author unknown.

By Christmas week, the turkeys we'd lifted off the Newcastlewest bus back in spring were bursting out of their feathers. Twelve in all: one for the Mullingar crowd, one for Newbridge, nine promised into Hourihan's in Clashganiv, and the biggest lump of a bird kept back for our own hungry table.

After the dinner, my father pushed back his chair and eyed the pair of bucks opposite him, Jackie and Joe.

'Come on, lads. There's work to be done, and 'tis past time ye made yourselves useful. Big Bridie will be here to pluck, and if they're not ready, she'll be gone faster than a fox out of a henhouse. Up! Or we'll be left doing the whole bloody lot ourselves.'

They straightened a shade at being called men, swallowed the last of the tea, and tailed him to the turkey house.

'Right, Jackie,' says my father, hand to the latch. 'In with you now and bring out the first bird you can put a paw on.'

'And no *foul* play,' says Joe, his grin ready for trouble.

In goes Jackie — all bullock and no ballet — and the whole house of turkeys lifts its head from the mash. A cock on the top perch gave a gurgle like an old harmonium, and Jackie froze, one foot half-forward, the courage gone sideways in him. He snatched for a neck with the speed of a scalded cat, missed it, and set the lot of them flying for the corner in a feathered hiddle, eyes bright as marbles and talkin' gobbledygook about his character.

'No one could catch them feckin' turkeys,' he roared, half-panicked, half-insulted. They'd have the feckin' eye out of your head in half a second.' And seeing Joe smirking, he let another volley fly, louder again, as if noise alone might save his pride.

Better a live coward than a dead hero, you could see him decide, and away he darts for the door—straight into Big Bridie herself, who'd come early, apron on and Woodbine parked in the corner of her mouth.

'Steady on there, boy,' says Big Bridie, squaring him up with a grin. 'I'd have thought you braver than that.'

'Brave me arse,' pants Jackie, feathers stuck to his brow like bad dandruff. 'Them feckin' turkeys are half-mad. They'd blind you in the blink of an eye, so they would."

Joe smirked but said nothing, knowing full well his own turn was coming and it might not look much better.

Big Bridie, God help her, tried to smother the laugh tickling her throat. She was young once herself and knew what it was to be made a show of in front of an audience.

But Jackie wasn't done. His temper rose with every feather clinging to him. 'Go on, Joe, if you're so feckin' clever. Show us how it's done, you feckin' eejit!'

Joe only grinned louder. He hadn't opened his mouth, and yet his silence alone drove Jackie to distraction.

'Feckin' this, feckin' that—' Joe finally sang back, 'till someone boots the feckin' cat!'

At that, my father burst, laughter shaking him the same way it did the day Paddy Barry was chased round the haggard by a swarm of bees, bawling, "Help! Help! Help!" But that's another yarn for another pint.

'Enough now,' Big Bridie said, stamping a Woodbine butt beneath her heel.

My father caught the two lads by their elbows and drew them close, lowering his voice like a man about to impart wisdom from the ages.

'Hold on there for God's sake, boys. Let the dog see the rabbit. Why d'ye think the fox is the cutest rogue in creation?'

'Why?' says Joe, innocent as butter.

'Feck's sake,' mutters Jackie.

'Because,' says my father, eyes narrowed, 'you'll never see a fox stomping about in hobnails, announcing himself to the hens. No, he sizes the thing up. He bides his time. He strikes when they're least expecting it. That's why he eats while the hens sleep. So—are ye men or mice? Go in there again and bring me out a bird, or there'll be no Christmas dinner for the pair of ye.'

'Hens, foxes, mice…' Joe muttered. 'I thought we came for turkeys.'

'Feck's sake,' Jackie said under his breath.

He stood there, turning it over. If Big Bridie spread word around the parish that he'd bolted, he'd never live it down. They'd be calling him "chicken" till Easter. Better to risk the scratches of a turkey than the jeers of a schoolyard. He squared himself, muttering "slowly, slowly, catchy monkey," and slipped back inside.

But no sooner had he crossed the threshold than his legs turned to timber and his tongue dried to leather. The turkeys, huddled in the corner like conspirators, gobbled in chorus, daring him to come closer.

'Go on, we haven't all day!' bawled my father from outside.

'I'll do it if you're too scared,' called Joe, sweet as vinegar.

Jackie braced himself, step by step, till one bold bird broke rank. It strutted round him like a cocky peacock, wings flaring, as if to say: *Come ahead, boy, and we'll see who's the man here.*

From somewhere inside himself, Jackie found a scrap of courage. Pride is a great motivator when you fear being the parish joke. By hook or by crook, he'd show Big Bridie and everyone he wasn't the coward they thought.

He forgot all my father's sage advice about foxes and patience, shut his eyes like a man facing the gallows, and charged headlong into the corner. Feathers flew, turkeys lifted in panic, and Jackie's hands flapped at thin air.

So he tried Plan B, which was the same as Plan A, only with less thought. Eyes clamped shut, he clawed at whatever came under his fingers — and by some miracle, he staggered out into the daylight clutching a squirming bird under his arm, breathless but triumphant.

My father took the turkey cool as you please, pinned it under one elbow, stretched its neck between finger and thumb, and with a twist, the matter was ended. Simple. Clean. Final.

The first is always the worst. After that, the lads lost their fear. One by one, the birds were carried out, necks pulled, and soon the barn held a silent row of turkeys hanging like Sunday coats.

Then Big Bridie took over. She was a good-natured soul, though the Woodbines had her chest wheezing, and a hearty laugh left her red about the gills. She plonked the biggest bird across her lap, its purple head swinging, and set to work. The feathers came away with a dull rip, drifting round the kitchen, till her hair was powdered white.

She dropped the feathers into the old tea chest — the very same chest Jackie was penned into as a baby to keep him out of mischief. The down rose like a snow shower, clinging to her hair, while the Woodbine smoke curled about her till she wheezed like a tired bellows. Later, my mother would haul the chest down, stuff the feathers into a Ranks flour sack, and some woolly head would sleep soft on them for years to come. Even the wings weren't wasted — singed at the joint, they'd serve as dusters.

Big Bridie, wiping sweat and feathers from her brow, handed Jackie a few plumes.

'There's your first feather in the cap, boy,' says she. 'Get your father to point another with the knife and you'll be writing letters like Lord Goff himself — and that's no small honour, even for the likes of yourself.'

By dark, a full regiment of turkeys hung naked in the barn, purple heads dangling, while Big Bridie went home wheezing, wrapped in her own fog of Woodbine smoke.

The next morning, I strolled around the yard, thinking it would be an easy day. What could go wrong?

The roar of my father answered.

'Out, you dirty pup! Who left the bloody barn door open?' he roared, bending for a stone and letting fly. It struck poor old Rex with a thud, and away he tore yelping, tail tucked tighter than the field mouse Mick Mullane stuffed in a matchbox the day of the thrashing.

I looked into the barn like a clown. Two of the turkeys were mangled, half-eaten, feathers strewn, Rex's guilty feast plain as day.

'What kind of eejits am I rearing?' my father roared. 'If there was one brain cell between ye, it'd die of loneliness!'

The trouble was, I was the only one in sight, so the blame landed square on me. Long practice had taught me to hold my tongue in such storms, and I slipped away before his fury found new fuel.

The loss left him in a quandary. Two birds short of what he had promised, he faced a choice: disappoint Hourihan's in Clashganiv or disappoint the relations in Mullingar and Newbridge. And if anyone was going without turkey, it would never be the relations. For fifteen years, the train had carried birds to their doors, and my father would sooner go without shoes than break that tradition.

So he went down to Clashganiv himself, held his hands up, and explained the sorry state of affairs to Mrs Hourihan. She was practical. Turkeys can't be conjured out of thin air, she said, and she'd find them elsewhere. With that, our own Christmas dinner — which had been hanging by a feather — was saved.

You'd think that was torment enough for one Christmas, but no — with our crowd there's always a twist in the old gizzard, another calamity waiting round the corner. What should've died quietly in the barn sprouted legs, found its tongue, and went walking up the road in hob nail boots. And that's where the next chapter of foolishness began.

The two buckos — my father's name for them, and apt at that — were as proud as peacocks the same evening. Didn't they parade up the road to Katie's, chest out, bragging about the heap of birds they had dispatched? You'd swear they were butchers to the gentry in the big house, the way they carried on.

Now, Katie had a prize turkey of her own, fattening in the shed under the big sycamore.

The sycamore tree — God blast it — where we lost a small fortune playing pitch-and-toss to that robber up the road. A man that'd skin his own mother, only he'd no one left to make the tea.

And sure, the lads, God help them, offered their services free, gratis and for nothing. What's a poor woman to do in the face of gall like that? She took them at their word, foolishness or fondness— and I'll leave it to yourself which it was.

'I always said your father had a sensible head on him,' says Katie, folding her arms the way a judge folds his file before sending a man down. 'But if he's putting his faith in the two of ye, I'll have to revise my opinion. Sure, it's like watching a solicitor pleading for a thief that's thirty-five convictions to his name. In and out of jail so often he could meet himself on the doorstep — going in as he was coming out. Guilty as a fox in a henhouse, and the lawyer still walking away with his fat fee. That's the kind of case your father's after taking on, trusting the pair of ye.'

'They're all dead and plucked at home, sure 'tis child's play,' says Joe, chest out like a bantam cock squaring up to a gander. 'Ask Big Bridie if you don't take my word for it.'

'I was going to ask Don Tarrant,' says Katie, lips tighter than a purse on Fair Day.

'We'll manage it, no bother,' says Jackie, hopping up like a pup with two tails.

So off with the pair of them to the shed. And Katie — God be good to her — half-admired the way they shouldered in bold, when only the day before they were flying round the yard like scalded cats.

But wasn't it written in the stars — or written in muck, more like — that between shed and kitchen, Jackie got a notion. Some half-witted classmate of his — the sort that'd know everything and understand nothing — had sworn blind he knew a foolproof way of killing turkeys. His father, says he, was a pheasant plucker, and he himself was a pheasant plucker's son… and you know yourself the rest of that blasted tongue-twister. He swore it was easier on the arms and softer on the conscience.

Back they barrelled into the kitchen, the turkey flapping and one wing stretched over Jackie's shoulder like a devil's cloak. Joe, cool as a curate, asked Katie for the loan of her sweeping brush. She gave him a quare, dangerous look that would curdle fresh milk, but handed it over all the same.

Down he laid it on the floor, solemn as rolling the red carpet for the Bishop on Confirmation Day. The two of them bent their heads, whispering like fellas hatching a robbery. Jackie muttered, Joe nodded, and the pair of them grinned the grin of men about to disgrace themselves.

'What in the name of God are ye cogar-mogaring about?' says Katie, her eyes narrowed to slits. And for a full moment she wondered — as did we all — what misfortune of Providence had the world slipping into the hands of eejits like these.

Jackie planted his boot on one end of the brush, Joe on the other, the turkey's head wedged beneath. Do you see the picture? Katie turned away, crossing herself, muttering twoul'd be the death of herself if Willy walked in on it.

Joe, arms full of flapping feathers, hauled at the body like a man dragging a stubborn calf. Jackie pressed harder on the brush, the turkey's eyes near bursting from its skull. 'Twas the quarest sight you'd ever see — and never wish to see again.

Then the chain of goms snapped at its weakest link. Joe pulled too hard, and the head came clane off with a tear — the very same as when Fat Joe Lane the time he bent over and split the arse of his trousers straight up the middle. Enough to shame any self-respecting man, only Fat Joe was born lucky: he hadn't an ounce of shame to lose.

The head rolled across the flags, eyes half alive, still hunting for the body it had lost. The head lay still, but the body took off.

I swear to the man above, the carcass staggered round the kitchen like it was after a feed of pints and a bag of crisps down at Harty's pub, spraying blood up the dresser, across the flags, and halfway down the hallway as if bent on redecorating the house in red for Christmas. The two amadáns ducked and dived, cursing and praying in equal measure, blood and feathers flying till the whole place looked like a botched operation in the County Hospital. At last, the bird, minus its body, flailed once more and collapsed in a heap like a sack of spuds.

Katie screamed to the Sacred Heart, hand to her mouth. Joe went white as a winding sheet, tripped over the carcass, and cracked his skull off the dresser. Jackie stayed planted, foot on the brush, eyes like moons, wondering which parish would hang him first.

'Ye pair of amadáns!' Katie shrieked, and in her fury walloped Joe while he was still sprawled on the floor — a bit much, you'd say, but that's what bad luck and rage will do to a decent woman.

'What sort of trick is that to play on me? Do ye want to put me in the grave?'

The lads, chastened, hung the bird proper, set a pan for the blood, and poured out apologies as fast as the blood had run. Katie spat curses and blessings both, scrubbing the floor as though to erase the whole business.

And then — as if the house hadn't had its fill — in walked Willy, boots clattering, eyes bulging. He stopped dead at the carnage.

'Sweet Jesus, what's after happening? I turn my back two minutes, and the place looks like a slaughter. When I catch them two clowns—'

But he never did, for the pair were already gone, fleeing down the lane like thieves with the moon at their backs.

Word of it was at our fire before the day was out, and my father was like a blue-arsed fly for days after. The two buckos kept well clear. Best not to tempt fate.

That night, while the two amadáns shivered under the blankets, waiting for the headless turkey to march up the stairs, the rest of us slept easy. Christmas was saved, dinner was certain, and we had a new story to last through the years. For all the feathers and the fury, it proved again what we already knew: pride is the fattest bird of all, and the first to be plucked.

And then, as if the world remembered itself, a calm returned. Fires were banked, tables cleared, and a stillness crept in that only Christmas Eve can bring. Candles were set in windows everywhere — one for the Holy Family, and maybe one for those who never made it home.

The Candle in the Window

Christmas Eve arrived like an ominous warning. The wind sharp as a hayknife, the clouds hanging low and mean. Not quite snow, not yet rain, but that horrible in-between dampness that clings to your clothes and whispers, 'There's worse to come.' After feeding the cattle, my father, never one to sit idle, said he was taking the pony to the forge for reshoeing.

I invited myself along, as you would.

When we reached the forge, the usual Christmas Eve suspects were already there — ponies tethered to the wall, horses shifting from hoof to hoof, and only the sound of hammering ringing off the anvil like a church bell.

My father glanced at the forge door. Sparks flew from the chimney, the red coal slack glowing under the bellows — the only light in the place. Black Paddy, the smith, was hunched at a hoof, paring and shaping, soot clinging to every inch of him. He dipped a red-hot shoe into the water barrel, and the hiss that followed was like Aunt Anne's bacon hitting the pan.

By the look of things, we'd be waiting a while.

"The poor man's lungs must be in an awful state," my father muttered, "and as for his pillowcase — I wouldn't like to see it."

"And what about his underpants?". I thought to myself, smiling..

He tipped his head toward Josie's pub.

"We'll warm ourselves while we wait," he said, and off we went.

Across the road, Josie's pub windows were steamed up and glowing. The real business of the day was already well underway.

Inside, the place was half-full and warming fast. The fire blazed, paper decorations drooped from the ceiling, and sprigs of holly poked out from behind picture frames — one showing a harvest scene with a reaper and binder, another a Fair Day in Mallow. A strand of tinsel, half-melted to the mantelpiece, looked like it had survived a few Christmases already.

My father took a stool at the bar beside a man with hands like shovels and arms you could hang wrought iron gates off. A proper farmer's build — pure brawn and not an ounce of fat, despite the daily diet of hairy bacon and curly cabbage.

"A ball of malt, a pint of your best porter, and a lemonade for the young fella," my father said, like he was reading from the gospel. "When you get a chance, Missus."

They fell into talk easily, the way a small community does— the kind of pub talk that jumped from funerals to ferry tickets without a breath in between. Who had passed on since the last Christmas, who was leaving on the first boat to England, and who was still holding a grudge from the Civil War.

And Dev up there in the Áras now," said the big man, lowering his voice. "The country'll never heal with that face preaching down at us from on high — and give it time, he'll be on every stamp in the land, and we'll be made lick him before we can post a letter."

"Collins was the man," my father said. "Only for—"

He trailed off. Even in a half-empty pub, you had to mind your words.

People were mostly civil — but the old lines were still there, drawn deep. Things were raw, and memories were long. Half the country still voted one way — and the other half never forgave them for it.

At the end of the day who can say who was right or wrong!.

Then a shout came from near the fire — and you should have heard it.

"Ah, for God's sake, Mister Kelleher — would you stop that dirty old habit! How many times do I have to tell you?"

It was Josie. And there was no joke in her voice when she let loose.

The old lad had hacked up a spit and lobbed it straight into the flames, without a thought or a care.

Josie looked to the ceiling and muttered, "Sweet Jesus, keep me from losing my temper — or I'll crucify him one of these days. Dirty, filthy old bugger."

The old man said nothing. Not in the least bothered. He just let her blow off steam, knowing full well he'd do it again before the evening was out.

One look at him told you that.

Around the bar, conversation buzzed — locals and emigrants, back for Christmas and eager to remind everyone of the life across the water. The visitors wore clean suits and stiff collars, shirts that never got the slap of a cow's tail, and shoes that had never stepped in cow shite. They were only too happy to show how well they were doing. Some were barely a wet week in London and already talking in full cockney. Still, you could tell — their hearts were half stuck in Kerry or Cork. And maybe, just maybe, it was all for show. Pride has a way of dressing things up when the truth's too bare.

There's money to be made, mate," said one, holding court with a pint of porter in one hand and a John Player sticking out of his mouth.

'Mate' — now there was a word you'd only hear when the lads came home for Christmas, fresh off the boat and full of stories.

"You'd be a fool to stay here diggin' spuds and milking cows for some old slave driver. Over there, on the buildings, you'd earn in a good week what'd take a month here — and that's on a slow job."

He leaned in, eyes shining, enjoying the attention.

"And Saturday nights, lads, you're in the Galtymore — packed with women, wall to wall. The talent's unreal. No priests lookin' over your shoulder either, not like here, with their long faces and longer sermons. You live your life the way you want — no one to say boo to a goose."

He took a slug from his pint and stamped out his cigarette butt under his heel.

"I've fifty fellas under me — our own lads from Cork, plus Mayo, Wexford, the whole bloody map. The old governor's a decent skin, even if he is from Cavan — he'll give a man a break. If things keep going right, I'll buy a little farm here someday and have a few fellas working for me instead. Just say the word and I'll have you sorted. Maureen in the post office has my address. I'm heading back over in the New Year, so if you're thinking of a change, you'll find me here before I strike for the boat."

He sounded like a man in the money, and every word of it had half the pub thinking of ferries and fresh starts.

It was tempting, right enough — a wage you could post home, a chance to walk away from dead-end labour. But then again, there was the mother at home, the sick brother, the father who'd sooner die than ask for help.

Things were never as simple as they sounded in pubs.

After a time, a boy came through panting from the forge.

"She's done," he said. "Mister Murphy says her shoes are on and waiting."

My father took the last slug from his glass, then ordered a crate of Nash's orange and lemonade — our once-a-year treat, reserved for Christmas or wakes — along with a bottle of whiskey and a bottle of Sherry to collect later.

Out on the road, we led the pony home on foot. Her hooves rang out on the freshly tarred road — clip clop, clip clop — and for a moment, it felt like something from a storybook.

That night, the house had never felt so warm or so cosy. The Stanley range roared, the cast-iron kettle hissed and spat, and the black pot gave off a steady scent of mutton boiling. My mother was in full ritual mode. She'd taken an Afternoon Tea biscuit tin, covered it in wrapping paper, and turned it into a crib. Inside, she arranged the little plastic figures — the sheep, the donkey, the three wise men. The baby Jesus wouldn't be placed in the crib until morning.

Billy got the honour of lighting the Christmas candle in the front window — red wax, melting, twisting and crawling down its stem. It was to welcome Jesus, Mary, and Joseph.

My mother, wielding the Holy Water like a farmer with a budget sprayer, nearly drowned us all. Then, the lemonade bottles were uncorked with a hiss, and the biscuits were passed around like communion wafers. It was USA biscuits on Christmas Eve — the plain ones — the good *Afternoon Tea* was kept for Christmas Day.

That night, she made her stuffing — breadcrumbs, pimento, a few odd spices, and her secret ingredient. Whatever it was, it was the best stuffing ever.

"If I told you," she said, wagging the wooden spoon, "I'd have to kill you."

The turkey, all twenty-one pounds of it, lay on the table like a small calf. She stuffed it with both hands, muttering to herself as she worked.

"Yes, mam, no mam, mam if you please. Is it up the duck's arse I stuff the green peas?" Billy said, grinning.

"Who told you a thing like that?" my mother snapped back, with a look that could fry an egg.

Before bedtime, she soaked the marrowfat peas overnight and dissolved two big lumps of jelly in a bowl, preparing them for the next day's dessert along with the sponge trifle.

When bedtime came, we knelt before the candle and the Sacred Heart, said the Rosary under threat of death, and hung our stockings above the range. The smell of soot, turkey, and tinsel filled the air. There was hope, if not full belief.

The wind was blowing up, and looking out through the gable end window and across the fields, I could see the snow starting to fall. I didn't care if the cold lino froze my toes off.

I never in my life saw anyone as excited as Mikey. He was glowing with anticipation, like the candle in the window.

I just hoped it all worked out for him. That's all there is to be said.

That night we slept with half an ear for sleigh bells, half an eye on the chimney, and full hearts — waiting to see what Christmas might deliver.

Morning came with the smell of the Stanley Range fired up, the turkey roasting, the crackle of wrapping paper and the cry of "who got what." The excitement and disappointment. It was the same chaos every year, and we wouldn't have traded a minute of it. After all the rushing and preparing, Christmas itself arrived quietly — nothing fancy, just the glow of a house alive with love and noise.

Christmas Day

The next morning, we were all up before it even got bright. Outside, a fine fall of snow had gathered, and someone's footprints were already tracked through the driveway and into the stall — likely my father, out to check the cows and throw them a bit of hay.

We galloped down the hall past the parlour and nearly burst the kitchen door off its hinges — like we were possessed by something. And we were: hope.

But for some — for Mikey — that hope was quickly dashed. He was going around with a face as long as a wet week. Santa, the mean article, hadn't brought him what he'd asked for — a Meccano set he'd seen in some magazine. And Mikey, poor crater, was trying to work out what he'd done wrong. What rule he'd broken? What prayer he'd missed.

The older ones, you could tell, had stopped believing altogether. And the rest of us were starting to suspect that the red fella with the long white beard had his favourites, and none of them were in our house.

I yanked my stocking down and reached inside: a bar of chocolate and a plastic tractor that had seen better days

— and maybe better children. It looked like it had spent five years welded to a snowplough at the North Pole.

Mike had already vanished into the barn, muttering about "that pile of junk" like a man on the edge of a nervous breakdown.

Billy, the golden child, got a wind-up dog that marched rhythmically across the floor as if it had somewhere important to be. But even that wasn't perfect. The poor mutt was missing an eye, its back leg twisted, and its matted fur stained in places best not spoken of.

As for me — well, as I'd suspected, there was no sign of my little red bike. Just a plastic tractor. The same one as last year. I hoped the little fecker, wrapped up in his velvet-collared coat and riding *my* red bike, fell off.

I must admit, I looked on with a mix of feigned admiration and pure — well, let's call a spade a spade — begrudgery.

As for the older ones — the doubters and cynics — Santa didn't even bother. They got socks and a bar of Bourneville. You couldn't argue with the logic.

Mother was up before us, as always. She had lit the range and slid the beast of a turkey into the oven — had to break its legs just to make the monster fit. Every ounce of twenty-one pounds. She handled it like she was launching a small ship.

Outside, the frost was biting. The road to Mass in the snow was the best — or so we told ourselves. We shuffled along, crunching snow underfoot, pelting each other with snowballs, half-frozen all the while. Breath puffed in the air, knees knocked in short pants, and teeth chattered in time like reciting the Rosary.

Religion, if nothing else, was an endurance test.

Each house we passed had a single red candle glowing in the front window — a silent prayer, a welcome for the Holy Family, or maybe just tradition clinging on for dear life.

At the church, the crib was set up under the gallery — straw, Baby Jesus, three wise men, sheep, a donkey that had clearly seen better stables, and a few angels strung to the roof. The place smelled of candles and cotton wool.

Visitors stood at the back, arms folded, sizing up the locals like cattle at a fair — shiny suits, clouds of Old Spice, and accents that would confuse a horse. Down the seat, a young one — all perfume and pretence — sat in a mini-skirt. Back from England, not there a wet week, and already the talk of the parish over Christmas.

"What's the world coming to?" hissed the woman behind me, as if she herself was the guardian of decency.

Mother and I took a pew halfway up, and I found myself wedged between her and a woman so round she could have been issued by the yard. But by God, she radiated heat, and I was glad of it.

The choir started into *Gloria in Excelsis Deo*, and as usual, one voice — a well-known parish missile — launched two words ahead of the rest and refused to come back—no names needed— statute-barred or not. Everyone knew the culprit.

The priest was in good form that morning — no sign of the usual fire and brimstone, no pounding the altar, roaring that we were all destined for Hell unless we repented, fasted, and practically died before we lived. Still, you could tell even that day's good humour might've been hanging by a thread.

Around the church, a few children had brought their new toys to Mass. One very small lad — barely up to the pew rail — started acting up. For a moment, I thought the priest might actually stop the whole proceedings and order the poor woman and her child out — and on Christmas Day of all days.

He paused his sermon once or twice, threw a look their way — that sharp, slow turn of the head only priests and schoolmasters truly master — and you could almost see the calculations behind his eyes. But whatever went through his mind, he held back. Maybe he realised it wouldn't look well, roaring down a young mother on the day that was in it. Especially not one who'd dolled herself up for Mass, set the fire that morning, most likely peeled a few spuds, and scrubbed the kitchen floor, and was now just trying to dote on her child for five minutes in peace.

And sure, what harm, really, if the cratereen let out a squeal or two? Isn't that what children are meant to do — for God's sake?

With Mass over, the congregation poured out into the crisp Christmas morning. Steam rose from mouths, and people gathered in tight little groups outside the church

— coats pulled tight, hands shoved into pockets — exchanging greetings, gossip, and the odd grumble about the weather or the world.

Just then, God forgive me, I got a great giggle watching the priest nearly take a tumble on the icy snow. He barely kept his footing, but his missal skidded away and landed face down in a snow. He kept his head down with embarrassment and hurried away, nearly falling again in the process — and sure, it's never nice when the laugh is on you now.

My mother stopped to talk to a woman she hadn't seen in a while. "And what did Santa bring you, young man?" the woman asked with a smile full of manners, an accent from the city. "A second-hand plastic tractor and a bar of chocolate," I muttered. "Isn't that lovely, all the same," she said — the kind of reply that tells you she knew it wasn't, but was trying to keep things light.

They went on chatting. I caught snatches — someone "awful lonely since it happened." Then Mrs O'Herlihy joined them. Wasn't her only son heading for the boat just after the New Year?

"What was all the old fighting for back then," she said, "if we can't even keep our own at home?" "And what kind of year has she to look forward to?" said the other. "But sure, you have to let them go," came the reply. "They have their own lives."

It wasn't exactly festive, but that was life for some — even on Christmas morning. Maybe now, too.

I spotted a few of my pals and broke loose — talk of toy guns, cowboy suits, and magic sets. Then one of them — a lad so pious he'd nearly genuflect in a puddle — proudly wheeled out a brand-new red bike.
I was mad as a goldfinch caught on a whitethorn, ready to kill on the spot and damn the consequences. That was my bike. Or should have been.

You'd wonder sometimes about Santa's priorities. Maybe Jackie was half right to stop believing. A plastic tractor and a lump of coal weren't all that different when you thought about it.

We trudged home after the greetings and the gawking, boots dripping snow, noses red, and stomachs hollow from the wait. The day felt as if it were only just beginning.

And sure enough, the moment we stepped in the door, the smell of turkey had already taken over the house. It seeped into every corner, even your thoughts. The radio played carols and a special Christmas edition of *Hospital Requests*. *Old Moore's Almanac* lay open on my father's armchair, with *The Holly Bough* and a half-finished mug of tea on the chair beside it."

The cap guns were already going off — that sulphur stink hanging in the air like gunpowder after a skirmish. My plastic tractor hummed across the lino floor, its wheels buckling under the weight of excitement.

Then Mikey burst in from the barn, holding up a twisted contraption he'd fashioned from the leftover Meccano. It looked like a steam engine crossed with a bicycle pump, but the pride on his face made it a masterpiece.

By dinnertime, the smell of roasting turkey had grown almost unbearable. The beautiful brown skin glistened, and you'd nearly attack it with your bare hands.

My father placed the monster in the centre of the table. Immediately, chairs scraped back as we scrambled to get our feet underneath. Mother had dressed the table with a new linen cloth that had never seen daylight before. She called it "the good one" — not like the usual pages of the *Examiner* with a pot of spuds dropped on top. We knew better than to treat it like savages and risk spatters and stains.

Mother carved the turkey with surgeon-like precision, while filling the plates like she was the head of the I.C.A., loading each one with potatoes, carrots, parsnips, marrowfat peas, thick gravy, and her famous stuffing — the kind that could make a bishop swear and go back for thirds.

"Joe, say grace," she said, as we hovered with knives and forks at the ready.

Joe, who had the subtlety of a sledgehammer, blurted:

"Father, Son, and Holy Ghost — whoever eats the fastest gets the most."

Silence.

You could hear the tick of the Cuckoo Clock. Mother drew breath through her nose. My father stared at Joe, weighing up whether to kill him or laugh.

Then — slowly — the corner of his mouth twitched. He smiled.

That was Christmas for you. One second from disaster, then pulled back by the skin of its teeth.

We ate like condemned men. The turkey, the stuffing, the trifle, the jelly, the biscuits — all of it gone in a blur of elbows and seconds.

For a few blessed hours, all was forgiven.

The incident with the curate was forgotten. We'll say no more about that. The smashed ware on the back kitchen dresser — gone- we won't mention that either. In fact, we'll let all of it Rest In Peace.

Mother leaned back in her chair, eyes soft, cheeks pink, and smiled as we roared and teased and passed around the lemonade. For once, there was peace, or at least something close enough to pass for it.

Later, my older brothers played records — Elvis, Buddy Holly, the usual suspects. We sipped the last of the lemonade, cleaned out the biscuit tin again, and picked turkey from the bones like scavengers.

By nightfall, we were full, wrecked, and drifting off in chairs, still half holding our toys and fresh memories. The candle flickered in the window. The radio faded to static.

It wasn't perfect. But it was ours.

And for that one long, happy, half-chaotic day — we were exactly where we were meant to be.

.

By Christmas morning, the excitement had settled into something quieter. Not everyone got what they wanted — some sulked, others shrugged, and a few found ways to make the most of what they got. There was always one who took it further, though — the sort who'd turn disappointment into discovery. Every house had its Mikey.

Little Mikey's Invention

As I mentioned, poor Mikey didn't get his Meccano set. His face was like a wet week on Christmas morning — but some children don't sulk. They plot. Not every child gets what they wished for, but some get ideas instead. And that's a far more dangerous thing altogether, especially if the child in question is called Mikey.

It was Christmas Eve night, and for weeks before, Little Mikey had talked excitedly about all the pictures of trains, tractors, and trucks that filled the pages of *Meccano Magazine*. The one he had seen in the shop—the steam engine set—kept him awake night after night. It was the very same one Santa was bringing him for Christmas.

Mikey's father was always good with his hands. He spent hours in the barn workshop repairing broken machinery or replicating bits of equipment that others would have discarded. It was just as well—his wealth never amounted to more than a rattle in his pocket.

Mikey wanted to be just like his father. His eyes grew wide at the thought of breathing life into the Meccano bits and transforming them into real, life-like machines with form, function, and wheels. And once he'd made one thing, he could take it apart and make something entirely different if the notion took him. He was already held high in his father's esteem, but once his father saw the train sets, tractors, and trucks he could build... well, that would be the icing on the cake. One day, Mikey would be his father's trusted assistant and share in the secrets inside his father's head. Mikey would be a great inventor—and people from all over the world would marvel at the brains that thought up such machines.

A snowstorm blew up on Christmas Eve and drifted against the windows. Livestock sheltered in sheds, munching hay. Mikey's mother lit all three fires in the house. It might have been freezing, but under the blankets and topcoats his mother found to keep him warm, he felt cosy. It was pure magic—just like the scenes on the Christmas cards that hung over the fireplace.

That evening, just before bedtime, his mother said to him:

"Listen here now, Mikey. You can't be expecting too much—Santa has very little money this year, and sometimes he only brings what he can afford. Sometimes, there's nothing more certain than disappointment."

"I've been good, and I know Santa won't let me down," Mikey replied, though a bit confused by what she'd said.

The wind whistled in through the draughty old windows. Gusts rattled the frames, as if threatening to blow the house down. The curtains ballooned and floated with each blast.

Little Mikey couldn't sleep with the excitement, and a troubling thought entered his mind:

What if Santa gets blown off course?

If the big man can't fix the weather, he might never see his Meccano set, and all his dreams would be dashed. Then again, Santa lived at the North Pole, and they always had bad weather up there. Besides, Mikey had never heard of *anyone* not getting something from Santa. Even bold children got something—maybe just a lump of coal in their stocking or a bar of chocolate—and something, anything, is better than nothing.

He remembered what his best pal, Big John, had told him. He said he'd even stolen a florin from his mother's purse off the top of the wardrobe—and after all that, Santa was *still* bringing him a fantastic big train set for Christmas. Big John had never lied to him before, not since the priest gave him a severe penance for throwing stones at Donal Burke's corrugated iron roof. It took him hours to say the twenty Our Fathers, twenty-five Hail Marys, and fifty Glory Be to the Fathers.

Confusing thoughts swirled in Mikey's head. Why did Santa bring big toys to some boys in class and not others? Tom, who sat next to him, got a flashy bike last year. Mikey only got what was left in the bottom of Santa's bag—a wind-up dog with three legs and one eye. Mikey's father named him Lucky, and everyone had a great laugh.

He wondered why his mother had said what she said—and why she'd put a big doubt in his head. He couldn't find an answer. Still, he reasoned, he had been good all through the year and tried even harder to make his goodness great.

Lying in the dark, he stared at the luminous statue of Our Lady and prayed inside his head that nothing—no matter what—would disturb the safe passage of the man in the red suit, whom he expected to arrive, come hell or high water.

Mikey tossed and turned all night. Finally, he curled into a ball, covering his head with the bedclothes to distract himself from the storm, which grew fiercer outside. Then, he heard a noise on the roof over his bedroom. Could it be Santa's sleigh landing? Would he possibly come down the chimney *in his bedroom*? Frightened, he covered his head again—just in case it was Santa.

By half-past five in the morning, the slender thread that held his patience together snapped. He threw aside the bedclothes and stepped onto the cold linoleum. Barefooted, he crept down the hall. One false move, one floorboard creak, and his father's snore would morph into a savage growl.

He tiptoed past the parlour and into the kitchen. There, his eyes met the sparkle from the shiny Christmas cards, lit up by the fading embers of the fire. The wind rose and fell; the open chimney drew great creaking drafts, threatening to suck the whole kitchen skyward.

Mikey flicked the light switch—nothing. He looked at the electric clock. It had stopped three hours earlier. The house sat in silence.

He crept towards the tree and found the presents beneath it. One by one, he pulled them toward the firelight. At last, he found the one with his name on it:

"To Little Mikey – Have a lovely Christmas. From Santa."

He ripped the paper off in unrestrained excitement—but paused. The cardboard box was wrinkled and faded. The cover was torn at the edges. The sparkle drained from his eyes as the tattered box revealed its contents: a jumble of straight and bent metal strips with chipped paint and a packet of screws wrapped in brown paper.

Even the colours of the pieces didn't match the steam engine on the box.

However good his imagination was, it was no match for the mess masquerading as Santa's Christmas present.

His spirits sank. A lump welled in his throat, threatening to choke him. He could no longer hold back the tears. They rolled down his cheeks as he sat, dejected, on the súgán chair by the fire. The worthless box of junk lay scattered on the floor, mocking him. Finally, exhausted, he fell into a deep sleep.

Morning arrived. The storm had abated. A thick layer of snow blanketed the yard. The sheepdog's prints traced a path in and out of the back kitchen door.

Mikey awoke to a hand tugging his shoulder.

"Wake up, Mikey, wake up."

It was his father. His sleeves were rolled, collar turned in, ready to shave before first Mass.

"What are you doing here at this hour, little man?" he asked, looking into Mikey's bleary eyes. "I see Santa came and brought you what you wanted."

"He did not," Mikey moaned. "It's the worst feckin' Christmas ever. He's the worst Santa ever. And I was good! Look at that pile of junk. I'd have been better off with a lousy lucky bag."

The great expectations that had kept him awake all night were in ruins—like the scattered Meccano pieces on the floor.

His father saw the disappointment plain as day.

"We'll have a closer look after Mass," he said gently, "and see if we can make sense of the pieces."

Mikey went outside. The fierce winds had given way to calm stillness. He saw fallen trees, loose iron sheets, and roof slates outside his bedroom window. The drenched sheepdog came to greet him. For his trouble, he got a kick—sending him yelping back to the hay barn.

Instantly, Mikey felt sorry. He followed the dog to the barn, and there, in the hay, he told him his troubles. And the dog listened.

When his father came back from Mass, Mikey was still sulking.

"What's the matter here?" he asked. "Surely you're not going to let a little thing like that ruin your Christmas?"

"*Little?*" Mikey snapped. "That's a pile of junk! I'm not even going to try to make a steam engine out of it. It's impossible! Nothing makes sense. Santa can stick the whole lot—where the Kerry man stuck his sixpence!"

His father ignored the remark.

"I've a bit of a conundrum for you," he said. "Some people have everything—and still they've nothing. Some people have nothing—and yet they have everything. It's about how they value things. Your disappointment is only a challenge to your imagination—a test of how determined and inventive you are. See the old paint chippings? That's what I call *character*. And character develops from life's experiences—like the wrinkles on your old man's face.

"You have loads of parts. Nuts, screws, everything you need. The only thing missing is a pinch of imagination, a dollop of improvisation, a pound of patience, and a mile of perseverance."

Mikey sat, stuck like a boot in muck. He couldn't lift himself from where his spirits had fallen.

"Listen, Mikey," his father said. "Nothing changes by standing still. A motor car is no good until it's moving. Come on now. Take all that stuff out to the barn and see what you can make. I'll bet you'll even surprise yourself."

For a while, Mikey said nothing. But eventually, he gathered the Meccano pieces and went to the barn.

He scratched his head. Finger at his jaw.

"What can I make from all these useless pieces? What if I bend a few? What if... no. It's supposed to be a feckin' steam engine."

Still, Rome wasn't built in a day. He stood back from the bench.

Why would Santa give a good boy a jumble of junk? That's not what Santas do.

Then he remembered his father's words: *imagination, patience, perseverance… improvisation*—whatever that meant.

And then another thought struck him.

Maybe there *is* a steam engine in all those parts—just not the one on the box.

Slowly, a design formed in his head. Bit by bit, the parts came together. They clicked like a jigsaw. One piece matched another. Until, at last, a faded multicoloured steam engine stood on the bench—twice the size of the one on the box. And he still had pieces left over.

He felt proud. Well—sort of.

He returned to the kitchen, where his father was reading the paper.

"Come here a minute, Dad," he said. "I've something to show you."

"Oh wow! That's fantastic," his father said. "It's even better than the one on the box."

"I wouldn't go that far," Mikey said. "But it's not too bad. And I've loads more pieces to make other stuff."

The bright eyes and broad smile returned to Mikey's face. He hugged his father.

That Christmas, Mikey learned a lot about being a great inventor. How to make the most of what you have. How to deal with disappointment. And how from that disappointment comes strength.

In the days that followed, Mikey took the steam engine apart and built all sorts from the pieces. He was no longer limited by someone else's imagination. He could see things in his own head—and make them real.

He and his father spent hours talking about what he'd build next.

Although only four feet tall, Mikey felt like a giant in his father's opinion of him.

The Christmas that started so badly turned out to be the best ever.

It was everything he hoped it would be.

After the turkey, the chocolates, and the fruit cake, the house grew heavy with food and idleness — but it never lasted long. By the next morning we were itching for fresh air and a bit of devilment, and what better excuse than St. Stephen's Day? We threw ourselves together as best we could — faces blackened, old net curtains for veils, caps pulled low — and off we went hunting the wren, hand outstretched for a few coppers and the odd sweet. We had no music, only a shaky recitation or two, but the fun was in the going. The proper wren boys with their bodhráns would take over the pubs that night; we were just the warm-up act, and happy to be it.

St. Stephen's Day

St. Stephen's Day was also known as Wren Boys' Day. The Wren is the smallest bird in Ireland, and few understand the meaning or tradition of Wren Boys Day and why this little creature should have been so ennobled. The story goes that, long ago in Ireland, boys would go into the woods to find and kill the Wren. That night, with painted faces and dressed in old clothes, they would parade the dead bird from door to door through the town, singing, dancing, and playing traditional music. In return, the people on whom such an honour was bestowed usually expressed their appreciation with some monetary reward for their troubles.

Early on St Stephen's Day, we took to our neighbours, Chrissie and Áine, to create a disguise so good that we would hardly recognise ourselves in the mirror. They blackened our faces with soot and clothed us in whatever was lying around, from moth-eaten net curtains and tattered topcoats to hats that even a scarecrow would reject.

The plans were made before Christmas to form a group of about ten to meet and do the rounds of our neighbours as far as our legs would carry us. Toots may have been our enemy when playing Pitch and Toss, but when hunting the wren, he was on our side because he had no shame and was an expert at making money. He would strangle his mother for a penny, everyone said.

Taking his advice that the early bird catches the worm, we set out early that morning. Our master plan was to enthusiastically caw a few verses of Jingle Bells and follow with a rhyme about the Wren, the King of all birds and then extend our hands in grateful anticipation of undeserved appreciation.

Mary Moran's was the first stop on our tour. We walked calmly to her front door, totally unlike the times some of our group robbed her orchard and took off like hares when being chased by her dog snapping at their heels. Mary answered her door after a few light knocks, and we immediately assaulted her with the first verse of Jingle Bells, which we sang in glorious disharmony.

Fearful that she might have to endure another verse, she shouted.

'Stop, Stop, Stop now, boys. That'll do. I'm nearly demented from listening to that bloody jingle bells all through Christmas.'

Respectful of her wishes, we stopped and waited. Then she looked at Toots in the front row and beckoned him closer.

'And who are you now? Come here and let me have a glake at you.' Toots stepped forward, and Mary stood staring at him, trying to figure out his identity.

"I'm Jerry Mullane from Ballybrack," says he, bold as brass. "And these here are my neighbours from back the road."

Mary wasn't long cutting the legs from under him. "Indeed, you're not," says she. "I'd know them curtains on your back anywhere — and the net to match! They're Áine's, off her gable-end window. The very ones she threw out after her poor husband died and she came into the money. God rest the man. Wouldn't he get the right hearty laugh if he saw what became of them now?"

At that, my brother Joe nearly killed himself trying to hold in the laughter. The poor divil was prone to nosebleeds at the best of times, and the strain of it burst a vessel. He wiped the blood away with the corner of the same faded curtain tied round his head — a fine advertisement for Ballybrack couture.

Before Mary could open her mouth again, our self-appointed leader, Toots, struck up the chorus, dragging the rest of us in after him like a parish choir on its last warning.

The Wran, the wran
the King of all Birds
on St. Stephen's Day
it was caught in the furze,
up with the kettle
and down with the pan
give us a penny

to bury the wran.

'Take that.' Mary said as she handed a few threepenny bits into the palm of Toots' hand.

We expressed our thanks to Mary and headed off to the next house.

'Why did you say you were Jerry Mullane?' I asked.

' You'll see, you'll see.' Toots replied.

By evening, our paths had crossed with several other wren boy groups armed with Bodhrans and Melodeons. We were lucky to have taken Toots' advice about the early bird catching the worm.

The occupants of some houses seemed to have taken flight that day in fear of having to part with a few pennies. Some tried to scare us away. One had even taken the log from around the dog's neck, where it had hung for the past three hundred and sixty-four days. Others simply drew the curtains and ignored our persistent knocking on their door. All the occupants who were *not in* but in seemed to forget about the telltale sign of the plume of smoke coming from their chimneys, the kind of smoke you wouldn't get from a half-dead or quenched fire.

By late evening, I had devoured all that I carried for sustenance, and my legs felt like lead in my boots. Toots' early bird tactics had paid off handsomely, yielding a fine haul of silver and brass. We counted up and divided the spoils. My share stretched from the tip of my middle finger to the end of the lifeline in my palm—

Seventeen shillings and three pence.

Then, after distributing the loot, Toots said.

'Remember, lads, you asked why I said I was Jerry Mullane.'

'Yeah.' We replied in unison.

'Well. It was quite plain that most people didn't recognise us, except maybe wheezy Joan but she's suspicious of everyone anyway. As they say lads—
make hay while the sun shines.' He continued with a big smirk across his face.

His plan was to alter our disguises and put different people in the front of the group. Anyway, the darkness would be our ally for another few hours. So, without a dissenting voice, we headed off for another few hours in the darkness, and despite a few suspicious looks, we increased our takings almost twofold.

When we returned home that evening, we found mother with her heart in her mouth from worry that we had fallen prey to the pooka or the long-wailing cry of the banshee. My father gave us a more frosty welcome home.

'I hope you didn't shame us.' He said.

'Shame us, never met him.' I replied.

That night, the Dromcollogher Wrenboys entertained the many pubs in the village with real music. The bare skin of their knuckles, beating rhythmically against the taut skin of the goat, produced a rapturous sound that transported people to the most primitive corners of their being. The hat was passed around, and the patrons rewarded real talent in appreciation. The Wren that nobody saw had the finest of wakes and would again resurrect himself like Lazarus the following year.

But not all nights ended in laughter. In the hush that followed the revelry, you could almost hear life drawing its quiet lines again — the reminder that joy and sorrow share the same roof. For every cheer in the pub or chorus at the door, there was always one house where the light burned low for different reasons.

And To Her Bed Untimely Sent Her

It had been bitterly cold all over Christmas — frost one day, hail and snow the next. The shed that once brimmed with firewood, turf, and coal was now half-empty, the lot drawn up the chimney in a swirl of smoke. The Black Stanley range roared feverishly, though it gave out more sighs than heat. On top of it, the cast-iron kettle bubbled and hissed, its lid rattling as it spat boiling drops onto the hotplate. There, the little beads danced a frantic jig before vanishing to nothing — like lemmings off a cliff.

"Come on, Moscow," my father said. "We'll go for a little spin to Uncle Gene's."

Moscow — that was his nickname for me when he wanted a bit of help. It went back to the days when the Yanks and the Russians were at each other's throats, threatening to blow the world to smithereens. Why he chose that morning to take me along, I'll never know. Mikie was usually his companion, unless the chilblains had him hobbling like a bishop with gout — though he was far too young for such ailments. Whatever the reason, I wasn't waiting for him to change his mind. Opportunities like that, once missed, seldom came again.

I sprang up and tore straight for the back kitchen to grab my coat, but in the excitement of it all, my enthusiasm was quickly reined in. A slick sheet of ice lay waiting just outside the door, and I — with my coat half on and half off — landed square on my arse. Ah, the tailbone: the most delicate piece of equipment a man owns, at least until it's tested.

My father nearly doubled over laughing.

"One look before you is better than two after you," he grinned, as if my downfall was the finest bit of entertainment he'd had since Christmas Day.

I swallowed my pride, rubbed the insulted spot, and followed him out to the little grey Ferguson parked at the top of the yard. Still smirking, he pulled a coarse rations sack across the battery beside the seat for me to perch on.

After a few splutters and coughs, he let the tractor roll down the fall of ground, dropped the clutch, and the old Fergie burst to life in a puff of black smoke. Seconds later, we were rattling down the road, faces flayed raw by the icy wind.

At Danaher's pond we slowed long enough to see a crowd of youngsters skating like demons across the frozen water. Mrs Danaher herself — fierce as ever — stood on the bank with a four-prong pike in her hands, roaring at them to clear off before the ice broke and swallowed the lot.

"Guess who'll get the blame if one of ye amadáns gets drowned? Muggins here, that's who!" she thundered.

No one paid her the slightest heed, and neither did we. My father only muttered that she was a woman best left alone — sweet as honey one minute, bitter as gall the next. A bit like the woman we'd be meeting at the end of our journey.

I turned once more to see her figure fading, still brandishing the pike and cursing them blue, until the bend in the road took her from sight.

A flash of red caught my eye across the fields — a fox, coat blazing against the snow, slinking away from Tom's place with a hen dangling from its jaws. Hard to begrudge him his prize in weather like this. Maybe he was the same rogue the neighbours cursed, the one wreaking havoc on the henhouses these past few weeks.

Further along, oblivious to all that, a man was bent double under a bundle of hay, plodding through the snow to feed his cattle — the weight of the world on his shoulders.

My father huffed into his cupped hands, purple with cold, rubbing his swollen knuckles as if to beat the arthritis back into hiding.

"The last time we had weather like this was in '47 — long before you were born," he muttered through the fog of his own breath.

I was thinking instead of Aunt Nell's big open fire, and the Binchy sweet cake she'd surely kept back a few slices of from Christmas. Though with Nell, good humour was rarer than hen's teeth, and you'd be a fool to bet on her mood.

We rolled into Gene's yard, my father steering the tractor toward a slope in case it later needed another downhill run to coax life from the battery. Nothing's more wretched on a bitter day than a tractor that won't start.

The yard itself was an ice rink, waiting to whip your feet from under you. Thick icicles hung like daggers from the cowstall roof. The dung heap sat grey and crusted. Inside, the cows munched their hay and mangles, the odd bellow booming under the tin roof. In the hay barn, two cats lay curled together in quiet contentment.

Charlie, Gene's ageing Labrador, looked out from the barn where he'd made his permanent quarters atop the bags of rations beside Gene's Morris Minor. The old grey farm horse, still tackled to the butt, stood chewing patiently on a clump of hay by the frozen water tank, steam curling from his nostrils.

Then came the smell — yellow bacon drifting from Aunt Nell's kitchen, sharp and sweet. My belly gave its own bellow. With luck, she'd be in one of her good moods and there'd be sweet cake enough to go with the tea.

"Come here a minute," Gene called, beckoning my father toward the low stone wall that marked the line between his yard and the Geaney sisters'.

On the far side stood the old Geaney farmhouse, its sagging thatch sheltering Kate, nudging ninety, and her sister Annie well into her eighties. The roof was more sieve than shelter, and if the rain hadn't already found its way through, it was only biding its time — and time, for both roof and occupants, was in short supply.

Kate Geaney hadn't set foot in the Village for more than a dozen years. Frail as the thatch above her head, she was kept in touch with the world only by the monthly visit of the curate — a kindly man, never stingy with his time, though not above slipping a half-crown into his own pocket after prayers and a slice of apple tart.

"May the blessings of God be always with you," he'd murmur, pocketing the coin with the same hand that blessed her.

Gene and my father leaned together across the wall, trading thoughts in low tones. I loitered beside them, stiff with cold and wishing myself anywhere else. An icicle among icicles — that's what I felt like.

"I'm worried about the poor old angashores next door," Gene muttered, his eyes fixed on the Geaney house. "An awful bloody time to be on your own, never mind the two of them. The last I saw of Annie was yesterday morning. Out she came with the ashes, gathering a few kippins for the fire. That east wind would skin a cat. She was foostering about by the old pony-trap shed, and when she turned for the house, didn't she nearly go head over heels on the frost. God help her.

"Now, Nell and myself would gladly do the little jobs for her — any neighbour would — but that's not Annie's way. I called across, asked if she was alright, and offered a hand. Do you know the look I got? 'Twas as good as saying, *Mind your own business, Gene.* So I did. She skedaddled back in, and that was that. Odd as a bag of cats, that one."

My father inquired after her sister, Kate — everyone still called her by her maiden name, Geaney.

"Last I saw of her was her brother's funeral in Lixnaw — Easter twelve months gone. Not a glimpse since. What gnaws at me now is the chimney. No smoke at all since yesterday evening — and that's the very time it should be belching. There's something wrong; I feel it in my bones."

The talk of bacon and sweet cake shrivelled away. Just my luck — the one morning my father hauled me along instead of Mikie. Curse him and his blessed chilblains.

"She's probably just taken to the bed," my father said, blowing into his cupped hands. "And who'd blame her in weather like this?"

A silence hung between them, broken only by the tap of his pipe against the stone. Words from an old school poem stirred his memory.

"Do you remember that poem we learned in school — about Old Betty, or some poor woman like the two next door?" my father asked.

"By God, then I do, and why wouldn't I. 'Twas bate into me," came Gene's reply.

"A coming storm your shooting corns presage,
And aches will throb, your hollow tooth will rage.

Her corns with shooting pains torment her,
And to her bed untimely sent her."

He paused, the words hanging in the cold air, then added softly:

"No fire to light, no strength to stir,
She pulled the quilt and disappeared."

He shifted slightly on the wall.

"Yes indeed," said Gene quietly. "The old bed can seem exactly the right place in weather like this. No shame in it."

"I remember too," he went on, "getting a clip round the ear trying to learn the bloody thing off for school. Education, they called it."

There was a touch of bitter nostalgia in his voice.

I always liked it when my father dropped a line of poetry or a scrap from a play. He had a saying for every occasion, always introduced the same way: *'It's an old saying, but nevertheless a true one.'* He'd never seen the inside of a secondary school, yet he could rattle off Shakespeare, Keats, and Shelley as if he'd been reared on them.

This time, with the weight of the moment hanging in the air, he murmured:

"As Lady Macbeth said — present fears are less than horrible imaginings."

I glanced over the wall. Annie's sheepdog stood whining, paws clawing at the door, before flopping back down on the step, ears low. His nerves were no better than mine. Up he'd get again, pace the yard like a mourner, then return to his post, staring at the door that refused to open.

"There's something rotten in the state of Denmark, I'm telling you," Gene said through a plume of smoke.

"There's something wrong, sure enough. We'd better do something," my father replied.

But Gene frowned. "Annie has her pride. She'd hate to think we were poking around. She'd be mad as Moll Bell."

The two of them drew deep on their pipes, tobacco clouds rising like incense at a wake. They stood there like village elders, weighing the problem as if chewing on a piece of sinewy beef.

"Pride was always Annie's curse," Gene said at last, his voice rising. "The worst of the deadly sins, if you ask me. Nell and myself offered a hundred times to do a job or two — even just to light the fire — and every time we were waved off. Dismissed with that look she'd give you. That bloody woman could never make a point without making an enemy."

My father blew out a long stream of smoke. "Blast it for a story. That's not pride — that's pure stupidity. It ruins the young and the old alike. The young rush headlong; the old sit too long and do nothing. Wisdom and foolishness bed down together in the same skull more often than you'd think."

"And what does that make us — wise or stupid?" Gene asked.

"Indecisive," my father quipped, smiling. "But at this moment, I'm not so sure."

Gene gave a half-grin. "There's herself skating on the ice, not knowing how thin it is beneath her feet."

"And isn't that all of us?" my father said quietly. "Only a matter of time till it gives way — and in weather like this, it'll swallow us whole."

I listened in silence, uneasy with the turn of the talk. Bacon and sweet cake were long gone from my thoughts; the signs were too plain — no smoke from Annie and Kate's chimney, no sound, no stir. The sheepdog rose again, scratched at the door till his nails rasped on the wood, then slumped back to the step, whining like a mourner.

Gene's voice broke the quiet. "Nell and myself have lived beside Kate for forty years, and Annie joined her more than twenty-five years ago. And I'll tell you something — we still know damn all about her."

"That's how it goes with some old people," my father said. "Spinsters especially. Private as you like."

Gene leaned heavily on the wall. "Annie's the last of the Geaneys — four sisters, none of them married. She nearly made it to the altar once, but the lad ran off to England and never looked back. Near broke her. Around the same time, Kate buried her husband, and Annie moved in. Misery loves company, they say. From then on, she trusted no one, shut the world out. It's a pity when life gives you a kick up the arse and you never get your wind back."

I felt sorry for the poor old woman after what I'd heard.

I thought of the times we'd mocked her, though never to her face. The picture in my mind was of a bent old woman in a black shawl, her back hunched, hand trembling on the blackthorn stick. My brother Jackie once summed her up with, "Here's my head, and my arse is coming."

My father shot back, "If you were half as clever with the books as you are with tomfoolery, we wouldn't be getting letters from the master telling us how smart you are not."

We'd roared laughing that day. Not so funny now. A few hot tears slipped down my cheeks before I could stop them.

The sheepdog scraped again at the door, frantic. There's truth in what they say about dogs — they never desert you. A bad day for you is a bad day for them too.

Just then, a hand tapped my shoulder.

"Put that coat on you, young man. There's no sense in catching your death."

It was Aunt Nell, standing there with a tray in her hands — three mugs of mutton soup and, God be praised, a slice of sweet cake for me. Nell was indeed a mercurial woman — no timing her moods — but this evening fortune leaned our way. They say adversity brings out the best in people, and maybe it had found her.

I cupped the soup in both hands, letting its heat thaw me. Behind the rising steam, I hid my face so my father wouldn't see the tears. With the sleeve of my coat, I wiped them away, passing them off as the cold's handywork.

The sky itself seemed to brood, the darkening heavens pressing down. I feared for something I couldn't yet name, and wished myself back by the Stanley range, listening to the kettle sizzle, instead of standing in this yard of dread.

Nell stayed with us as my father and Gene gnawed the problem back and forth — *will we, won't we, what if, if only* — chewing it to rags like two cows on the same cud.

Finally, Nell snapped.

"Listen here, the pair of ye — you're like two donkeys staring over that wall, talking yourselves into the grave. You'll have something else to chew soon enough, and it'll haunt ye all your days if you don't quit the talk and see what's wrong with our nearest neighbours, for God's sake. And while you're at it, that poor young fellow there will be frozen solid, and the three of ye will end up in graves yourselves with pneumonia."

Gene shifted, uneasy. "Ah, but you can't go trespassing on a body's privacy, Nell. Annie guards it like a dog with a bone."

"There's only so far you can carry a person's privacy," she cut across him. "Being a good neighbour comes first — and being a neighbour means action. To hell with all this privacy rubbish. Now, will ye for God's sake get on with it!"

Her words left a chill sharper than the frost. My heart sank. I prayed it was all just a nightmare — that any second I'd wake at home by the warm Stanley, the kettle spitting merrily, life safe and ordinary again.

Reluctantly, my father and Gene climbed the wall, not sure which was worse — Nell's growl or whatever waited behind Annie and Kate's door. I trailed after them, though not too close. The sheepdog rose once more, eyes fixed on the door, whining like his heart might break.

"That dog has fierce sense," Gene muttered. "He knows there's something not adding up. Do you remember the time the bull in the Well Field nearly finished Ned?"

"I do," my father said. "Like it was yesterday. Sure, Ned was never the same after — knocked the spirit out of him, what little was there to start with."

"I do indeed," Gene went on. "And it was a dog that saved him, same as this one's trying to save Annie now. Came scratching at our yard door till we followed him out. Found old Ned sprawled in the grass, half-dead and no notion of the world. The way this fella's carrying on, it puts the shiver up my back."

Gene thumped his fist against the Geaneys' door, the bang echoing like a drum.

"Are you there, Annie? Kate? Anyone?"

My heart hammered in my chest. No sound inside — only the dog's sad whine. Gene banged again, harder, but the silence only grew louder.

"Run round the back, boyeen," he called to me. "See if there's a window open."

The very thought turned my stomach. Broad daylight or not, I was rooted to the spot.

"Go on now — what's keeping you?" Gene barked again.

Where the hell is Mikie and his blasted chilblains when he's needed, I thought bitterly.

Still, somehow my legs carried me around the narrow space at the back of the house, hemmed in by the whitewashed wall and the gable. I stretched up on my toes, trying to peer through the sash window, but the panes were fogged with condensation, the net curtains stained and sagging. All I could see was darkness — and I thanked God for it.

Further along the wall was a smaller window, the frame half-rotten, a frosty cobweb stretched across it like a veil. It gave onto a narrow corridor dividing the bedrooms from the kitchen. One pane was missing, and through the gap a small hand like mine could slip in to lift the sash latch.

I turned to where Gene and my father hovered behind me.

"There," I said. "That's the only opening anywhere — and

I'm not going in. No way. I'll open the latch, and that's it."

Gene stuck out his chest, making a brave show of it. "Well then, nothing for it — I'll have to squeeze in myself. If I can."

Nell, arms folded, cut across him.
"Sweet mother of Jesus, what sort of an old eejit are you? You haven't a hope. You'd get stuck halfway and block the light for the next fifty years."

With that, she turned on her heel and marched back to her kitchen. I'd have given a fortune for an invite from Nell at that very minute. Oh, for the fire's glow, a rasher or two, and another slice of sweet cake.

Instead, I stood rooted, calculating the grim equation: one tiny window, one Gene with a backside the size of a haystack. There was only ever going to be one outcome.

Still, he gave it a try. Grunting and cursing, he shoved a shoulder through, then became wedged — feet dangling in the air like a turkey for the slaughter. My father shot me a grin, and I couldn't help but grin back.

"God forgive me," my father chuckled, "but you're the very picture of a square peg in a round hole."

Gene's muffled roar came back through the frame.
"You and that young buck can wipe the smiles off yere faces. There's nothing funny from where I'm standing."
To be fair, *standing* was generous — *dangling* was closer to the truth.

But as quick as it came, the laughter died. The dog whined at the door again — sharp, mournful — and the cold seemed to press tighter around us. Whatever lay inside, it would not be a thing to laugh at.

It felt like an eternity freeing Gene from the window. After much puffing and grunting, he finally wriggled loose and landed back on his feet, red in the face — a turkey cock in all his glory.

Gene and my father turned to me together.

"Would you give it a go again, Moscow?"

"Not a chance," I shot back, scurrying to a safe distance before they could press me.

But luck — which never deserts a man for long — arrived in the shape of my brother Joe. He came striding up out of nowhere, cheeks frosted from the wind. When Gene and my father explained the task, the colour drained from him faster than a pint down Big John's gullet.

It was no small dilemma: go in through the window and face the unknown, or refuse and be branded a coward for life. Reputation won out. With a leg-up from Gene, he squeezed through the pantry window. His boots hit the cold, black concrete floor with a thud, and he sighed — heavy as a condemned man.

"Good man, Joe," my father whispered.

Strange how people whisper in such moments — as if the dead themselves were listening.

"Have a look around the house, see what you can see."

Joe crept forward, step by wary step, until he reached Annie's bedroom. He lifted the latch; the door groaned, and a shaft of weak winter light fell across the washstand — the enamel jug and basin beside an empty iron bed. Annie's bed was dressed and neat. Empty.

He moved to the adjoining room — Kate's. His hand trembled on the latch. For a heartbeat, he nearly bolted back outside, but instead he pushed on. Another bed, neatly made. No one there. The cold in that room was worse than the yard outside — a chill that sank straight to the marrow.

He pressed on to the kitchen. Ragged curtains smothered what little light there was. A smell of burning hung in the air, turning his stomach. He drew the curtains — the same ones that had drooped there for thirty years — and the room filled with a pale, reluctant light. In the window stood a Christmas candle in a jam jar, burned down to its stub, sprigs of holly still around it.

He shoved the window open.

"Do you see anything?" Gene's voice barked from outside.

"Give me a chance," Joe muttered back.

"Leave the boy be — he's doing his best," Nell snapped, reappearing with a heavy coat for my father and a blanket for Gene.

My father stood silent, pipe in hand, breath steaming into the bitter air.

Joe turned from the window and took in the shadowed kitchen.

And then he saw what no young fellow should ever see.

A cold sweat surged through him, filling every vein and sinew with dread.

In the shadowy corner by the fire sat Annie — lifeless in her chair, head drooped onto her chest, legs charred where the flames had caught them. Opposite, Kate rested in her sugán chair, her frail hand still on the handle of the bellows, as if she had tried, in her last moment, to coax the fire that betrayed her.

He came tearing out the front door, screaming, his face blotched red with shock. He wanted to be anywhere but there — away from the sight that had invaded his young eyes. The air outside cut him like a blade, but never felt so sweet.

At that moment, Annie's dog slipped inside, nose to the ground, while Gene and my father followed quickly after.

Joe stood rooted, trembling, Nell's arm clamped firm around his shoulders. I lingered further back, afraid to know what it was that had sent him bolting.

Inside, the dog whimpered and circled the two lifeless women, then slumped beside them, his head low. After a time, as if recognising the hopelessness of it, he padded out again and collapsed on the doorstep. I went to him, knelt, and rubbed his head. In our grief, we found comfort in each other.

I couldn't bring myself to look inside. From the low voices of Gene and my father, I knew the truth was grim enough. Gene straightened—composed..

"We can't touch the bodies. The Gardaí will want the place as it is. I'll go fetch the Sergeant."

Off he went, shoulders hunched, down the road to the barracks — like a man handing himself in.

Nell hurried away and returned with a bottle of holy water. She sprinkled the cottage, in and out, like a woman disinfecting sorrow itself. Then she crossed herself, lips moving:

"May their souls, and the souls of all the faithful departed, through the mercy of God, rest in peace."

My father knelt with her, and together they said a decade of the Rosary as the light dimmed outside.

The Gardaí arrived soon after. With her shawl drawn tight, Nell turned to Joe and me.

"Come on, boys. Their souls are in Heaven now. Time ye had a bite. A bit of a fry and sweet cake will do ye better than standing here in the cold."

We followed her back to the warm kitchen. Joe sat staring out through the window, seeing nothing. I fixed on the fire — the flames leaping and twisting in the draught. My mind was full of shadows, none of them kind. I had no taste for fry or cake.

"What happens when you die?" I asked Nell, the words slipping out before I could stop them.

She looked at me kindly.

"When you die, everything is put right again. Like when you're worn out and only a good night's sleep will do. That's what happened to Annie and Kate. They were tired of living — and now they rest. May God be good to them."

My father appeared in the doorway and tugged lightly at my elbow.

"Time we went home, young men. More than enough for one day."

P.S.

There was never any official word on it. Still, for days after, the talk around the place was the same: that Annie, finding her sister gone, took such a fright she fainted away herself and slipped too close to the fire.

A sad end, people said — but God be good to them both.

And then, as happens, the talk moved on. The living turned back to their lives, the dead to their rest.

Yet life, stubborn as ever, pressed on. Grief gave way to gossip, and before long the talk turned to hounds, horses, and hunts. The same fields that had echoed prayers now echoed horns and hoofbeats. You might shake your head at the madness of it all, but that was country life — moving forward whether the heart was ready or not.

Tallyho

John Joe had a great grá for the outdoors. He loved the fields, the woods, the wild freedom of it all—where everything had its own place, its own rhythm, its own reason for being. Some days, the work was ordinary enough—sowing in the spring, reaping come autumn—but other times, well, there was magic in the land. The kind of magic only country people truly understand.

Now, back in the sixties, the rabbits had gone mad altogether. Multiplying like, well—rabbits. Farmers were tearing their hair out, watching entire rows of cabbage vanish overnight. Gardeners threw curses to the sky. Something had to be done, so it was.

In walked a cute Kerryman—Horan was the name—from Ballybunion way. A man with a tongue that could sell sand to the Arabs. He landed in the village one fine day and started spreading the word: a shilling for every rabbit, provided it was caught in good nick. And better still—he'd take the lot, no matter how many you brought him. Said they'd be shipped off to France, no less, to end up on the plates of the crème de la crème. "The finest Parisian parlours," he said, "will be scooping gravy over your catch."

Well, now—how could a young fella resist that kind of offer? International trade, like. At thirteen or fourteen years of age, they were barely fit to tie their laces, and here they were, exporters! Carpe Diem**,** the Latin master would've said—though none of them knew what it meant.

John Joe and the lads — all only teenagers with more nerve than sense — seized on Horan's offer like terriers on a bone. A few pounds for their leisure time? Sure, where would you get it? They schooled themselves fast in rabbit ways, scouting out the best haunts and runs. Before long, they'd settled on the double ditch of the Campaign Field and the Pump Field meadow, where it backed up against the Carty's wood.

Every Friday evening before dark, they set their snares, and every Saturday at first light, they were back, eager to see their catch. By the time Horan rattled round that evening, the rabbits were still warm and stiff enough for his shilling. Twenty shillings to the pound — not bad going at all for a bit of sport in the countryside.

Snaring was mighty craic and paid well, but it was nothing compared to the thrill of dazzling rabbits by night. At night, you could feel yourself turning wild too, honing the old hunter-gatherer instincts. The scrub rustled and God only knew what was in there: maybe a badger grubbing about, or a hedgehog snorting like a little pig, or an owl with his belly full of field mice, eyes glowing red-orange from the branches. Sometimes a bat skimmed so low over your hair you'd duck. Once they even saw a fox bounding a ditch with a hen clamped in its jaws.

Like the creatures themselves, John Joe and his pals were on the hunt for food — the very food, as Mister Horan reminded them, that would grace the tables of the finest homes in France. With a borrowed car battery and a clapped-out headlamp from a scrapped car, they stumbled over ditches and gullies, swearing under the weight of it.

When a rabbit crossed the beam, it froze, blind and panicked, darting left and right. Quick as you like, they grabbed it, a sharp chop to the neck, and hey presto — another shilling's worth into the bag. The night ended only when the battery, or the lads carrying it, gave out.

And when John Joe said "borrowed" battery, he meant it in the loosest sense. It came straight out of his father's Wolseley motor car. Many's the morning the old man swore blue murder when the engine wouldn't start.

Horan's rabbits, as it turned out, were served up as stew in restaurants. But after a few years, the great rabbit trade collapsed — myxomatosis, a filthy virus, all but wiped them out.

The countryside around Fadarsúl, all hills and hollows, was made for fox hunting—at least in the eyes of those who thought themselves bred for the saddle. The views were grand, and the ground soft under hoof. An English tradition, of course, handed down by the Landed Gentry—the well-fed, well-dressed and often fairly useless. It was a far cry from John Joe's modest roof, where the only red coat was black, the one his father wore to funerals and to Mass on Christmas morning.

Their farm happened to sit right between two fox coverts. One at Pluckanes, bounding their furthest field, and the other a mile away at Kilgawly, as the crow flies. A field gate joined the two. It was a quiet enough gate most of the year—but come January, it was a godsend for nervous riders hoping to avoid the deep watery dyke that had claimed more than one gentleman's dignity. Or worse, his hat.

John Joe, for his part, had long dreamed of riding with the Hunt. The whole drama of it—the bugler's call, the pounding hooves, the blur of the fox in the distance, the pack of hounds giving voice—he found it all strangely thrilling. But dreams are one thing; saddles and riding boots are another.

His rabbit-money wouldn't stretch that far. Saddlery wasn't cheap. And even if it was, the men and women of the Hunt weren't exactly known for welcoming local lads with open arms—especially not those without polished accents or polished tack.

Still, John Joe had made up his mind. Come hell or high water—or both—he was going to take part in that hunt. And to his way of thinking, he had every right. Hadn't they been traipsing across his father's fields for years, without so much as a by-your-leave? Sure, hadn't his father, in the name of good neighbourliness, turned a blind eye to the lot of them? If anything, they ought to be grateful. He wasn't trespassing on *their* land. If anyone was entitled to ride out, it was him.

And so his now-or-never moment arrived on New Year's Day.

The village was overrun: footpaths clogged with horseboxes, lorries, polished cars, and people strutting about as if their grandmothers had left them castles instead of cowsheds. The riders were dressed like something off a biscuit tin—scarlet coats, white jodhpurs, polished boots, riding crops flashing in hand.

For a country that spent eight hundred years trying to send them packing, we seemed to have kept a soft spot for their pomp and ceremony. Ah well—maybe there's no such thing as a classless society. But by Jove, there's plenty of the upper class who have no class at all.

A few of them even raised silver stirrup cups outside the pubs, sipping port and sherry with the solemnity of bishops at the altar. Stirrup cups, mind you—an old English tradition, meant as a genteel farewell before the ride. Half the crowd lifting them had barely the arse in their trousers the rest of the year, and here they were, posing as landed gentry. Everyone else in the village knew the truth, but sure let them have their moment of grandeur.

The ladies, God help us, some of them sat side-saddle like statues, as if Victoria herself had ordered it, stiff as pokers and twice as useless. The horses, for their part, were clipped and shining, manes plaited like schoolgirls off to their First Communion.

The hounds padded about in a tight pack, sniffing and snorting, their handlers murmuring instructions like schoolmasters on a cold yard. Everyone seemed to be waiting for something—a bugle, a toast, a signal from on high.

And then there was John Joe. His pony wasn't much for show, but she was hardy, quick on her feet, and knew every ditch and gap for miles around. She'd pulled the cart to the creamery more times than anyone could count. John Joe rode her bareback round the land, sure and easy. He trusted her—and more importantly, she trusted him.

That morning, he rose early, brushed her down till her coat shone, and mounted up. No saddle, no boots, no crop. Just a pair of wellingtons, an ash plant, and a grin. He trotted into the village like a man with nothing to prove and everything to claim.

As he ambled through the village, he passed clusters of finely mounted ladies and gents outside the pubs, sipping their stirrup cups like royalty on a break. Their accents floated through the frosty air, clipped and cultivated, the kind of tones rarely heard between Fadarsúl and Ballyglen. They had that peculiar way of speaking that suggested you were lucky to be in their presence.

One woman, perched side-saddle like a statue with a sneer, gave him the once-over and said with mock curiosity:

"And where do you think you're going like that, young man?"

John Joe looked her up and down, calm as you like.

"You could have a bad accident like that, Ma'am," he said, "with your nose stuck in the air and sitting the wrong way on the horse."

Not far off, a red-cheeked man with a face like boiled ham turned to him and growled:

"Listen here, my good man. You surely don't think you're going on the Hunt with that old nag—and no saddle to boot?"

"You don't need a saddle if you know how to ride," John Joe answered, steady as a priest at a christening.

"Let me tell you now," the man huffed, "there'll be no rescue for you when you land in the dyke. Perhaps next year, when you can afford a proper mount, eh?"

"Don't worry about me, Sir," John Joe said. "You'd be better off worrying about yourself."

The man's voice rose.

"Move along, you impudent brat, before I give you a lash of my crop!"

John Joe gave a crooked smile.

"I'd love to see you try", and as if to mock your man ", Eh!"

That might've gone badly only for a local man nearby—a sharp-tongued sort with no time for snobbery—who cut in:

"Don't waste your breath on the likes of him," he said to John Joe. " 'Tis a pity we didn't finish the job and turf out the whole bloody lot of them when we had the chance. Beggars on horseback, planters every one. Pennies looking down on half-pennies. You've more right to ride than that shower put together."

The ruddy-cheeked man scowled and moved off, not keen on tangling with locals who might take the crop off *him.*

Soon after, the Master's bugle rang out. The riders kicked into motion, hooves striking road and sod, the hounds flowing like a furry river. John Joe tucked in quietly at the rear, not keen to stir another fuss.

Fox hunting, he knew, wasn't always greeted with smiles and sandwiches. Plenty of landowners had no great fondness for the sight of high horses trampling through fields they'd worked with their own hands. The Hunt Master, to be fair, was an old hand at smoothing things over. He rode well out in front, both as courtesy and to get first crack at diplomacy should he meet a cranky farmer with arms folded and a pitchfork near to hand.

The fox, meanwhile, was no fool. A creature of habit and territory, he rarely strayed far from his den—especially not in cub-rearing season. The covert was meant to be a sanctuary. And it was… until the Hunt rolled in with all its red coats, brass bugles, and bloodthirsty tradition.

As was custom, a man called the Earthstopper had come the day before to block the escape holes. So when the riders and hounds reached Pluckanes that New Year's morning, they found the fox already cornered—pacing the undergrowth, ears twitching at every snap and rustle.

It was a pitiful sight. Like some poor slave in the Coliseum, buried to his neck in sand while the lions were let loose. The man can do nothing but stretch his head, open his mouth, and pray. And then Caesar, with a straight face, shouts down to him: *"Fight fair!"* The odds are stacked, the fight already lost. And here too, the fox never stood a chance.

What was a place of peace became a place of terror.

The hounds crisscrossed the perimeter, snouts low, eyes alive. Hooves squelched in the softened ground. Birds shot from the trees. Hares darted. The fox twisted and turned among the bramble, heart hammering, waiting for a chance—any chance—to break free.

Then—one hound yelped—another bayed. The scent was found.

From the brush, the fox leapt over the ditch, through frost-bitten field. A shout went up:

"Tallyho!"

The bugle sounded sharp and cold. The chase had begun.

One small fox. Fifty hounds. A stampede of half as many horses.

He made for Kilgawly Covert, head low, tail down, body stretched like wire. Maybe, if he was quick enough, clever enough, and lucky beyond reason, he might make it. Maybe the scent would break, or the hounds would falter.

But again, the odds were stacked sky-high against him.

John Joe, bareback and clinging by the seat of his muck-spattered trousers, did his best to keep pace as the hunt thundered ahead. His pony, God help us, was game and sure-footed, but no match for the tall thoroughbreds slicing through field and furrow.

At Scully's Glen, he spotted the ruddy-cheeked gentleman who'd given him lip back in the village. The man was now redder than ever, stuck on the high bank of a gully, trying to coax his glossy beast across.

Try one — no good.

Try two — a backpedal and snort.

Try three — disaster.

The horse bolted, lost its footing, and both man and mount landed head-first into the brown water with a splash big enough to baptise a parish.

John Joe trotted up and watched, grinning from above as the man climbed out—soggy, spluttering, and stripped of dignity.

"Can I help you?" John Joe asked, all innocence.

The man squinted, wiping mud from his brow.

"Aren't you the young chap I addressed earlier in the village?"

"That'd be me, alright. The fella with the nag. The one with no saddle. Funny thing now... look who needs rescuing—with a fine leather saddle under his backside."

The man scowled.

"Less of your cheek, if you please. Now tell me—is there another way out of this cursed field? And not a word of this to anyone, d'you hear me?"

John Joe smiled, pointed to a lower crossing, and even gave him a leg up for his troubles. The gentleman took off, his horse kicking up shame and slurry in equal measure.

Meanwhile, the fox — poor divil — was running for his life.

Across hedges and haggards he flew, his limbs stiffening, his lungs raw. The hounds were gaining ground, snarling behind him like a flood with teeth.

At the cross field, he stumbled into a crowd of onlookers. Startled, he turned—only to face the dogs again. Left, right, straight ahead—every route blocked by man, ditch, hoof, or hound. The whole countryside seemed to close in on him.

At the last ditch before Kilgawly Covert, one hound nearly caught him — jaws flashing. But fate, or wire, intervened. The dog tangled and cut himself on a barbed fence and fell back yelping. The fox scraped through into the brush, shaking, soaked, and half-dead with fear.

The hounds lost the scent, confused and circling.

When John Joe caught up, the Covert was swarmed: riders, hounds, onlookers — all waiting for blood.

Then he saw two men creeping into the wood with a crate under one arm and a snarling hound by the lead. Inside the crate: a ferret. And if you knew anything about ferrets, you knew what was coming.

They found an open den, fed in the ferret, and stepped back.

A few seconds later, a racket exploded underground — and a second fox burst out. Smaller, younger. A different fox entirely.

The hounds pounced.

John Joe watched, frozen, as they circled tighter and tighter — a noose of fur and fang. The young fox held his ground as long as he could, but the end was inevitable. He was pulled, torn, dragged in every direction — spirited, stubborn, and outnumbered. In minutes, it was over.

John Joe's face went pale. The excitement that had buzzed in him that morning drained like the colour from a bruise.

What kind of sport, he wondered, needs the death of a cornered creature to call it a good day out?

He turned his pony and rode home in silence.

That evening, back in Dan Twohig's bar, the riders gathered again. The day's work behind them, they raised their glasses — port, brandy, the odd pint — as if they were lifting stirrup cups all over again.

"To the one that got away!" said one.

"May he live to fight another day!"

"A lively little bugger," another chimed.

"One less fox to kill the old goose," added a third, to much nodding.

Outside, the village returned to its hush. The huntmen and huntwomen filtered off into the dark, satisfied.

John Joe washed down his pony in the yard at dusk, fed it and stabled it for the night. His father watched from the doorway.

"So," the old man said, "how'd the Ladies and Gentlemen of the hunt treat you today?"

John Joe didn't answer for a long while.

"They killed the wrong fox," he said at last, tidying himself up.

"They usually do," his father muttered and went back inside.

As Christmas faded, another kind of thinking took hold — the kind that comes when the days are short and the mind turns long. Do I go, or do I stay? The question was never far from any door. Some dreamt of new starts, others feared them; some left and made their luck, others vanished into silence. Those who stayed carried their own kind of courage — facing the same fields, the same faces, another year. The old year slipped quietly away, leaving its laughter and its ghosts behind, and the tide of life moved on — uncertain, but always forward.

The New Year's Boat

Like two sides of the same coin, Christmas could be the happiest and most miserable of times rolled into one. Some remembered the year fondly — raised glasses of whiskey and sherry, passed tins of biscuits and chocolates, and relived small glories like they were state funerals. Others wanted to close the chapter entirely, post the cards, eat the turkey, and get through it without crying into the stuffing.

That's Christmas for you. It didn't just mark the end of a year — it held up a mirror to it.

In the last slow, restful week of winter, people dropped in on family and neighbours. Some came with cake, others with grudges, and a few with nothing but silence. Old wounds were patched up or reignited, depending on the mood and the measure of drink. The wayward sons and daughters returned in coats two sizes too big, some scrubbed up in suits or powdered like film stars. A few of the daughters' friends came dolled up, bold as brass — trying not just to be seen, but to be someone else entirely. Some came to reconnect. Others just wanted a look at the town they left behind.

And of course, as always, the talk turned to resolutions.

"No more porter," said Joe, lighting his fourth fag. "I'll start going to Mass again," declared Nóni. And Maureen

— God help us — announced she'd stop judging people right after she judged every one of us to our faces.

Those earnest promises were often strangled at birth. Life was miserable enough without making it worse. And maybe, just maybe, that miserable so-and-so really was a miserable so-and-so. Everyone's human, after all.

But under all the laughter and leftovers, something else stirred — that low, familiar ache in the belly of the parish—the annual upheaval. Every year, a few more quietly decided: *There's nothing left for me here.* And so they left.

Some slipped away before the bells. Others boarded what became known as *The New Year's Boat.*

It wasn't always a real boat. Sometimes it was a ferry from Tivoli. Sometimes a train, rarely a flight, cos they were too expensive, or a borrowed coat and a lie about plans for January. But once they were gone, they were *on it.* They had left. And we had stayed.

Some of them would succeed — we knew that. They'd send back cards from Camden and pay slips from Slough. They'd come home the next Christmas with English accents and duffel coats, doling out Cadbury's Selection Boxes like saints. The neighbours would whisper, *"Didn't he do fierce well for himself?"*

Others would end up in the dumps of the big city. Dreams shattered. Cheques cashed straight into pints. They'd find themselves in Kilburn talking to the wall of a bedsit heated by hope and damp.

The streets of London weren't paved with gold. They were barely paved at all.

Still, the craic was good in Cricklewood. And the Galtymore Ballroom had hosted many great nights. None wilder than the time Larry Cunningham played there in '67 — a night still spoken of like the parting of the waters in the Bible.

But the music didn't last. For every lad dancing inside, another sat outside with a bottle, wondering when it all turned sour. And many cashed their cheques for liquor before the second verse even played.

Take Maureen — sharp-tongued, sharper-minded, and not to be crossed in either season. In summer, she'd march through the town like royalty, head high, hair perfect.

If someone asked her, "What does your husband do?"

She'd smile like she'd rehearsed it: "He's a painter, my dear. A good trade. Honest. Handy. He'll build us stairs by Easter."

But in winter, the wind knocked the shine off things. If someone asked her the same question. She'd sigh, knot her scarf a little tighter, and mutter: "He's a painter… God help us."

Because painting, like hope, was seasonal. In July, there was always work. In January, there was just the cold — and a half-tin of unused paint and used brushes.

Still, Maureen carried on. She always had a plan. Always had a prayer. And always had something to say about everyone else's shortcomings — especially her brother Mick.

Mick was another sort. Good hands, bad habits. He could mend a slate roof in a storm, but couldn't hold a job or a promise longer than a week.

One St. Stephen's Day, after a card game and two hot ports, he stood, zipped his coat, and said to no one in particular: "That's it. I'm for the boat."

The first card came from Holyhead—the second from Cricklewood. The third never came.

Some said he married a nurse in Camden. Others said he was spotted, down and out, stone drunk, talking to himself near a bridge in Kilburn.

Maureen never confirmed or denied. She just stopped putting his name on a quarter of Christmas cake. Eventually, she stopped glancing at the post altogether, didn't even notice the old clock he once fixed, sitting silent on the shelf. She'd given up. Sure, it takes two to tango, and he never showed up to dance.

People came back, too — sometimes with money, sometimes with guilt. There was a man who walked into Dan Murphy's after twenty years, and nobody recognised him until he said "a pint and a half one" with a strange mix of cockney and a farmer from near Carthy's Bridge direction.

He stayed a week. Promised to settle. Caught between the present and the past, he was back in Camden by mid-January, and he'd do the same again next year.

"It's a huge change of culture," someone whispered. "Here or there — they're lost in both."

And sometimes, quietly, when no one else was listening, you'd hear someone say: "I wonder… was it ever real? Or was it just a dream?"

Some carved a hearth. Some ate the snake. Success wore ties. The worn wore time. One dined on turkey. Another on rind and drink.

And the homesickness of our grandfathers — both of them — burned just as fierce in us as it did in them.

Back home, things rolled on.

The Mass was half full and half asleep. The fire sighed in the grate. Someone muttered, "At least the pints are cold." And the range gave off just enough heat to fool one into staying alive.

Still, the New Year's Boat sailed.

Maybe we all board it the day we're born. The journey starts out calm — a cradle on still water. But over the years, storms come. Winds shift. Some grow, others twist. Some capsize, some change course, some right the boat again. And sometimes the sea calms once more, lapping like memory on the shore.

Some rowed. Some drifted. Some collided with themselves.

That night in Dan Morley's, the place was half-empty, half-lit. Jimmy Quinn was asleep under the dartboard. Someone had stolen the head off the crib again, and the paraffin heater was ready to smother everyone wherever they sat.

In the quiet between songs on the jukebox, you could just make out the old ballad drifting from the back room —

"Oh Mary, this London's a wonderful sight..."

The volume, unnoticed, had climbed — or maybe the moment sharpened. Either way, the words struck the pub like a backhand: sudden, sharp, familiar.

A few heads turned. Faint smiles flickered, but nobody spoke. We'd all heard it before — the longing in it—the lie in it too.

Joe said nothing, just took a sip and muttered: "They never do mention the rent, do they?"

The song played on. *"But for all his great powers, he's wishful like me..."* And for a second, the whole pub seemed to listen — not to the words, but to what wasn't said between them.

Then Dan himself, polishing a glass near the heater, said it quietly but clearly: "Ah, sure, we all take the boat in the end. Just don't know when. One way or another, we're all in the boat already — travelling inexorably to a destination we know not where."

The fiddler slept. The ledger closed. And Maureen, now older, sat near the hearth with her feet up, watching the window for a brother who still owed her many letters or just one last one and a packet of fags.

"Ah, well," she said, rising to put on the kettle, "I might as well start the New Year and sure God is good"

Outside, the wind had softened. A new calendar hung on the wall—waiting. Waiting for the future, if there was one. And somewhere — across water, or memory, or both — the next dream was already stretching its legs.

Afterword

These stories were all stitched together from memory, myth, and the small truths we share in warm kitchens and smoky pubs. My parents never spoke much about how hard life was — they didn't have to. They were the lucky ones: they accepted their lot and never complained, except about the pains.

I'm sure they had their own quiet conversations, among friends and neighbours, about the turns their lives had taken — what they missed, what they carried, and what they hoped we might do better. That ache never quite leaves us. The New Year's Boat still sails, even if we no longer see it.

Thank you for reading.

About the Author

Maurice Brosnan grew up in rural North Cork, where family, neighbours, and friends shaped a lifelong love of story. His writing blends humour, memory, and Irish vernacular, capturing the voices and rhythms of a world that is fast fading.

He is the author of *A Life Unfolding*, *Whispers of the Past*, and the poetry collection *Long Shadows, Short Days.*

Although often asked if these stories are autobiographical, they are not memoirs — nor do they claim historical accuracy. They are stitched together from memory and imagination alike: snatches of talk, glimpses of people, half-remembered moments, and the bits and pieces of truth that life throws our way.

This is not his life story, but a truthful echo of what life once was — and of how it felt in the not-so-long-ago. In truth, everyone was telling a story, even if they didn't realise it.

Printed in Dunstable, United Kingdom